Multi-Orgasmic: A
B.

From the author:

Firstly, I want to extend my thanks to those of you that have purchased this anthology. I wouldn't be doing this without your support. Please bear in mind that most of the stories in this collection have been previously published in anthologies and online, but that I retain the right to publish them. A few of the stories are brand new and have never been released before. I hope you enjoy this collection of erotic short stories, and that you'll consider leaving me a review once you're done reading. Each and every review really helps me, and I'm very grateful. Thank you.

Happy Reading,
Lucy x

Table of Contents

A Problem with Authority

Private Jesse Bagnall glowered and muttered to himself all the way to the mess. He'd just been bawled out by Corporal Roxanne Grey—yet again—and he was getting seriously fed up of it. He knew he wasn't perfect in the drill exercises, but then nor were any of the other guys. It was like she was singling him out and aiming all her abuse in his direction. Being shouted at was to be expected in the army—it was almost part of the job description—but Corporal Grey's attitude was bordering on discriminatory, and he didn't know what to do about it. Especially without looking like a total pussy.

Spotting some of his closest friends at a table towards the back of the mess, he caught the eye of one of them—Matt Kay—raised a hand in greeting, then got in line for his food.

Several minutes later he loaded his cup of tea onto his tray along with everything else and headed over to where he'd seen Matt and the boys. Hopefully they'd take his mind off the Queen Bitch. They were always game for a laugh.

"All right, lads?" he said, sliding his tray onto the table and taking a seat.

There were mumbles of assent.

"Yeah," replied Ed Patterson. "You?"

"Yeah, I suppose."

Ed raised an eyebrow, and the other men turned their attention to Jesse, too. "Well," Ed said, "that wasn't very convincing. What's up, mate?"

Jesse sighed and ran a hand through his hair. "It's the drill instructor."

His friends exchanged confused looks. "Care to elaborate?" Matt said.

Not wanting to look like a wimp in front of his mates, Jesse changed his tone. But once he had, the anger took over him. "She's a fucking bitch, that's what!"

The confused expressions turned to surprised ones.

"I'm fed up of her treating me like a twat. I know it's her job to bawl us out, but she takes it too far. I do my fucking best, work my arse off, and it's still not good enough for her."

He barely noticed the gazes of his friends shifting slightly, and carried on regardless. "She definitely picks on me more than everyone else. As though I've seen sitting on my arse when everyone else is killing themselves to get it right. She's just being a complete and utter bitch. Bitch face fucking Grey!"

Matt cleared his throat, to no avail.

"You know what her problem is?" Jesse continued. "She needs a fucking good shag, she does. That might cheer the miserable cow up. Mind you, Christ knows what man would be brave enough to go there. She'd probably bite your cock off as soon as suck it."

As the red mist of his anger dissipated, Jesse finally clocked the reactions of the other men around his table. They weren't at all what he'd expected. Ed and Matt looked mighty chagrined, staring at a point over his left shoulder. Private Graham Pilgrim had actually put his head down and begun to bang it on the table.

A cold trickle of dread ran down his back, and he turned, wondering which of his superiors had heard his rant.

Fuck. It was none other than the target of his diatribe.

Corporal Roxanne Grey stood, her arms crossed, one high-heeled foot tapping on the floor. Her facial expression was as far from impressed as it was possible to be.

Coolly, she said, "Bagnall. Guard room, now."

Jesse's heart sunk into his heavy-duty boots, and he had to resist the temptation to drop his gaze to the floor. His buddies would never let him live it down. He had to do as the woman said otherwise he'd be guilty of insubordination, but he was going to do it in the manliest way possible.

Turning back to the table, he sneaked a quick glance at each of his friends in turn, hoping his expression looked irritated, not shit scared, which was what he really was. Standing, he left his lunch tray where it was and followed Corporal Grey out of the mess, across the yard and into the scruffy-looking building that was the guard room. God, the government really needed to put some money into this place—it certainly didn't give off the air of tough professionalism that the personnel were expected to show.

Opening the door, Corporal Grey stood aside and ushered him in, before following him and shutting the door behind them and twisting the lock. The room was empty. She moved to sit in a chair, and motioned him to take another one.

"I suppose you know why you're here?"

"Yes, ma'am. My unforgiveable words and actions back in

the mess." Now it was just the two of them, he could grovel as much as he felt necessary without worrying about losing face.

"Hmm. Yes. But actually, it's more the reasoning behind the words that I'm interested in."

"W—what do you mean?"

"You mentioned that you feel like I pick on you, more than I do anyone else during drill instruction. As though you're sitting on your arse, I do believe were your words."

Jesse fought the colour coming to his face, and failed miserably. "Y—yes, ma'am."

"Do I really make you feel that way? Or were you just having a whinge to your mates? Tell me honestly, please."

The anger had gone from her tone, and her expression was open, expectant. She really and truly wanted him to be honest. He opened and closed his mouth—not unlike a fish—a couple of times, before clearing his throat and attempting to form an answer. It didn't help that, now she'd stopped screaming at him and was actually being quite pleasant, he'd come to the conclusion that she was hot. Even in her army uniform, she looked feminine, as though she was hiding a delicious body underneath all that olive green.

"O—okay then. Yes, you do. Ever since you turned up to drill us in preparation for the parade, you've made me feel like a useless sack of shit. I know it's important, God do I know, and I want to get it right, but I really am trying my best. I'm giving this my all, and it seems as though it's just not good enough for you. Some of the other guys are worse than me, and you don't come down on them like a ton of bricks. Maybe just half a ton." He smiled weakly, hoping she'd realise he was joking.

A tiny smile played at the corners of the corporal's lips. "Would it make you feel any better if I told you why I'm doing it? Shouting at you more than the others, I mean."

"Um, I guess it depends on what you're going to say. I'm really not as shit as some of the other guys."

"I know. But..." She got to her feet and moved to stand in front of Jesse. Leaning down and placing her hands on the arms of his chair, she continued. "Let's just say I'm trying not to let my true feelings show. If people found out how much I want you, I don't think it would go down too well."

"W—want me? *You* want *me?*" His heart pounded, and his brain raced to keep up with what she was saying. Did she really mean what he thought she meant? Was there a way he could have misunderstood her words? He didn't think so. "You mean, like, want me in the sex way?" He knew his phrasing was ridiculous, but he couldn't think of anything better right at that moment. His brain was too fried.

Corporal Grey laughed, her blue eyes sparkling as crinkles appeared in their corners. It was adorable and sexy all at once, and Jesse's cock surprised him by hardening.

"Yes," she said. "I mean in the sex way. But I guess you know now why I've been behaving the way I have? Can you forgive me? I didn't mean to make you feel like a useless sack of shit. I'm sorry."

"Yeah, I can forgive you. But only if you make it up to me." It seemed his cock had taken over control of his mouth now, because as the words floated into the air, he realised he had no idea what he actually meant.

"Oh yeah?" Moving her hands to her hips, Corporal Grey adopted a saucy stance. "And how am I supposed to do that?"

Jesse cast his gaze about the room rapidly, hoping for inspiration. Thankfully, he spotted something that would serve his purpose perfectly. Standing, he gently pushed past her and retrieved the pace stick that was propped up in the corner. Designed for marking time in parades and similar, when it was open it formed a 'V' shape; closed it was just a wooden stick. One he could use to get his own back on Corporal Grey. And he really had to stop thinking of her as Corporal Grey, especially considering what he was about to do. She was Roxanne.

Turning back to her, he stifled a grin when he saw the look on her face. She obviously hadn't been expecting that. Pointing to a nearby table, he commanded, "Pull your skirt up to your waist and bend over."

"O—okay."

She sounded nervous, and he didn't blame her. Frankly, he was surprised she'd agreed. He was wielding quite an interesting weapon, and she was going to allow him to use it on her. Perhaps she was into a bit of pain. He'd soon find out.

Following her to the table, he waited while she summoned her courage, then lifted her skirt. His eyebrows nearly disappeared into his close-cropped hairline when he saw the skimpy black thong that had been hidden beneath her drab skirt. It bisected lovely pale, round bum cheeks, and suddenly he wanted nothing more than to pull the material aside and bury his cock in her warm depths.

First, though, Roxanne had some making up to do. "Ready?"

Pressing her hands to the surface of the table, she nodded quickly.

Jesse moved into the position he thought best and waved the pace stick around a little, to get used to the way it moved and balanced. He'd never spanked a woman before, never mind with one of these things. God knows why he'd even suggested it. She probably thought he was some kind of kinky bastard, now. Never mind, it was just a bit of fun.

Fun that was already making his cock throb and press insistently at the inside of his combats. Sucking in a deep breath, he drew his arm back and forth a couple of times, practising the correct angle to strike Roxanne's delectable bottom. He didn't want to accidentally whack the back of her legs, or miss utterly and hit the table.

Coming to the conclusion he could do this all day and not feel any more confident, he figured he should just go for it. Shifting his arm back once more, he then swung it all the way forward until the pace stick hit her naked skin. There was an interesting slapping sound, followed by a yelp from Roxanne. Milliseconds later, a red stripe decorated her skin. It looked kinda sexy, and as she hadn't screamed blue murder and run away or tried to kill him, he decided she could take it.

Lining up carefully once more, he laid another blow on her arse. It bobbed enticingly with the impact, and a red mark appeared next to the first. His cock was fit to burst. God, he hoped she'd be up for sex after this. Perhaps he oughtn't push her too far, just in case. He definitely didn't want to go and have to rub one out in his bunk.

Two more swings later and Jesse decided to change his tactics. The stick was fun and it probably hurt like hell, but it was damn unwieldy and he wanted to lay strikes on her faster and with more precision. There was only one thing for it—he'd have to use his hand.

Discarding the stick with more eagerness than he'd admit to, he reached out and stroked Roxanne's burning cheeks. "Okay for a few with my hand?" he asked.

"Yes." She was breathless, and sounded as though she was on the verge of tears, but if she wanted him to stop, she'd have said so. Corporal Roxanne Grey was no pushover, which was why they were in this situation in the first place.

Shrugging, he altered his position once more and whacked her right cheek. Then the left. If her skin hadn't already been so red, he was sure he'd have left handprints. Growing more confident, he slapped her harder, experimenting with a flattened hand, then a cupped hand, to see which made the best sounds or caused her to gasp more loudly.

Soon, he could take no more. His hand stung like fuck, and if he didn't do something with his dick soon he was probably going to come in his underwear. Raining a few more blows down on her for good measure, he then grabbed her by the shoulders, pulled her upright and spun her around.

Her face was red, her eyes wide. But she hadn't been crying, and she didn't look angry. In fact, she looked as horny as he felt, her eyes glinting and her lips parted enticingly. Taking advantage, he slanted his mouth over hers and kissed her with all the need and arousal he was experiencing, hoping like hell she wouldn't decide he'd gone a step too far.

Thankfully, she didn't. She returned the embrace, slipping her arms around his neck and kissing him back with a bruising ferocity. So it seemed she *did* like the pain. That was something clearly worth knowing. Their tongues brushed together, explored, tickled and fought until Jesse was dizzy with need. Pulling away, he gasped for air, then said, "Roxanne, I really need to fuck you, but I don't have a condom."

A coquettish smile taking over her lips, she replied, "It's okay, I do." She moved over to a bank of lockers, opened one of the doors and pulled out a handbag. Dipping her hand inside, she rummaged around a little and emerged with a foil packet.

"Wow, you're prepared." He couldn't hide his surprise.

"Wouldn't you be if you were one of the few women on an army base?"

"Touché. Now, shall we make use of it?"

"Abso-fucking-lutely. Get your cock out."

The woman really was full of surprises. Doing as he was told, he undid his combats and pulled his cock out, stroking it up and down a couple of times while she ripped open the packet. Taking the protection from her, he rolled it down his shaft carefully, then pushed on the base to make sure it was secure.

Shuffling towards the table, where Roxanne had now perched, skirt still up, legs akimbo and the gusset of her panties pulled to one side, Jesse was slammed with another massive wave of arousal. Her cunt was gorgeous. Hairless, swollen, pink and slick, he wanted to taste it. But that would have to wait for another time—if he was lucky enough to get one. For now, he'd give her the most memorable fuck he possibly could.

"Ready?" he said, gripping his shaft with one hand and moving the other around her back.

"Yes, Private, I'm ready. Just get on with it, will you?" Her words were harsh, but the look in her eyes told him that she was feeling as horny, as playful as he, and she really wanted to fuck.

Not wanting to disappoint, he positioned himself between her thighs, aimed his cockhead at her entrance and slowly pushed home. She was tight, yet incredibly wet, so he didn't meet much resistance as he penetrated her. And yet, she felt like a warm, slick glove around him, and if he wasn't careful, he was going to be in danger of premature ejaculation.

Slipping a hand between their bodies, he sought her clit, which was not difficult considering how large it was, distended with arousal. God, could this woman get any damn sexier? Stroking, pinching and rolling the flesh as he rocked in and out of her, he was determined to find out exactly what pushed her buttons so her climax would wring his own out of him. He'd come then, but not before.

Capturing her lips once more, he poured everything he had into pleasuring her. A long, hard, sensual kiss. Varying movements on her bud, and alternate fast and shallow, then slow and deep pumps of his cock. He'd find out what worked for her and exploit it to the extreme. In the meantime, he had to hang on to his own orgasm. He would not come until she did. Absolutely not.

Soon, he found the perfect formula. Suckling on her bottom lip, he pressed hard on her clit and fucked her fast and furiously. Her moans grew louder, then quieter as she remembered where she was. It wouldn't do either of them any good to get caught.

Suddenly, Roxanne's internal walls gripped him so hard he thought she'd rip his cock off. The pressure was intense, constant. Then she pulled her face away from his, yanked the collar of her shirt into her mouth and bit down as she tumbled into bliss.

Amazed, he watched her face go through a number of changes as her cunt gripped harder still, then released and went into a series of spasms, milking his cock. Shunting into her a couple more times, he let himself go with a sense of relief. Tingles shot from the base of his spine, leaving a line of fire running up his shaft and out of the tip as he came. He gritted his teeth to keep himself quiet, enjoying the immense sensations of his own climax and Roxanne's combined. He wouldn't have been able to hang on much longer, she just felt too damn good.

They held on to one another as they rode out their respective orgasms, and Jesse found himself hoping against all hope that this wasn't a one-off.

"Hey," he said gently, when he finally regained his voice. "You all right?"

Looking every inch as though she'd just floated down to Earth, she nodded, and grinned dopily. "Yeah. You? We all square? Have I made it up to you sufficiently?"

"Hell yeah." He pressed a kiss to her forehead. "So does this mean you're gonna be nicer to me now?"

"Uh, no. People will notice. I'd rather carry on being a total bitch to you, then I can keep fucking you in private and no one will suspect a thing."

"Oh, well, when you put it like that... be as bitchy as you like."

"I thought you might say that."

Grinning, Jesse voiced his next thought. "So, you got another condom?"

Chasing

You've heard of those storm chaser folks, haven't you? The ones that go out seeking tornados and stuff so they can do scientific research on them? Well, I'm like them. Only I chase orgasms, not tornados. And I'm not interested in research—scientific or otherwise—just the extreme pleasure each and every climax gives me.

I guess you're wondering why I've compared myself to a storm chaser now, aren't you? After all, orgasms are two-a-penny, right? Not for me. I used the comparison because my climaxes are as unpredictable as the weather, and so elusive that I have to chase them relentlessly, using specialised equipment.

I was nineteen when I had my first orgasm, and it was courtesy of my brand new vibrator. I'd had several lovers by then, but none of them had even come close to making me come. It didn't mean that the sex was crap—far from it, in some cases—but for some reason, my clitoris would simply not co-operate. It became a constant source of frustration—for both myself and my sex partners—and I was convinced there was something wrong with me. I read books, I searched the Internet, and soon discovered that I wasn't alone. According to many sources, the problem was psychological, not physical. They also said that if I couldn't make myself come, then how could I expect anyone else to?

I tried. Really I did. I watched porn, read dirty books, pulled out the lube and masturbated until my fingers went stiff, my wrists ached, and my lady parts were sore. I ended up more frustrated than ever, and eventually headed into a sex shop and purchased myself a rabbit vibe.

The first time I used it, I came so quickly that I barely knew what it felt like. I was left breathless, with my cunt spasming wildly around the shaft of the toy and a flush that ran from my chest up to my cheeks.

Oddly, my first emotion was relief. So I *could* orgasm, I just needed something battery-operated to help me out. It was better than nothing, and once my clit had recovered from its sensitivity, I switched the toy on again and teased my body into a second climax. That time I was more able to savour the sensation. I can't think of a word that truly captures how it was. Think divine, heavenly, blissful;

times that by ten and you're somewhere in the right region.

From then on I was hooked. I now knew exactly how wonderful it felt to climax, and I wanted more. Knowing I was physically able to come from clitoral stimulation took a weight off my mind. I thought perhaps it would clear the mental block that was preventing me from coming by my own hand and with partners. Sadly, that wasn't the case. Lots more toy-free masturbation and several sexual partners later and I was still orgasm-less.

Thankfully I always had my vibrator as backup, and every time I went grocery shopping I added batteries to my basket. I came perilously close to turning into a teenage boy. Not literally, of course, but in the locking-myself-in-my-room-and-going-through-lots-of-tissues way. I just got addicted to the feeling that so many women take for granted, and pushed my body over the edge again and again, marvelling at how completely amazing and mind-blowing it was, each and every time.

Now, though, I have a much better handle on things. I know that I *can* come, and that the ability isn't going to disappear. I hope.

It's getting harder. Compared to the first time, when I came so quickly I hardly knew what had hit me, it's growing increasingly more difficult. In the months and years since that eye-opening moment, I've bought every type of sex toy going. More rabbit-style vibrators, dildos, wands, bullets, remote-controlled knickers... you name it, I've bought it. I should probably have shares in the battery manufacturing companies, I'm spending that much money with them. The trouble is, no matter how wonderful and powerful these toys claim to be, there's only one that can make me come.

My trusty rabbit. It alone can tease my stubborn clit into submission, bring that delicious tightening sensation to my abdomen, make my pussy flutter and give me climaxes so extreme that I writhe on the bed and yell so loud my neighbours probably think I'm being murdered.

My first one broke, you know. I panicked. The thought of never being able to come again struck terror into the very depths of my soul. I literally dropped everything and ran to the computer to order another one, exactly the same. Thankfully they still stocked that particular model.

I don't know what I'll do if they discontinue it. Maybe I should buy several and keep them in storage, just in case.

I know it sounds crazy. Excessive. But can you imagine

having one single thing, just *one* way of making yourself feel on top of the world? And to risk it being taken away? You wouldn't, would you? It's unthinkable. I'm trying new things all the time, just hoping that there's something, or someone, else that will shake my clit into submission and break me into tiny fragments of ecstasy. So far, there's nothing or no one. But I'm having fun trying.

So that's why I continue to chase climax, with my specialised equipment. Because I won't give them up. I won't. I *can't*.

Maybe I should try therapy. I'm beginning to think it'll be cheaper than all these damn batteries.

When Dreams Come True

Chapter One

When Karen awoke with a start and shot upright in bed, she realised her boyfriend of eleven months, Peter, was staring at her incredulously.

"What?" she said, defensively. She'd only just woken up, what could she have possibly done wrong? Stolen the duvet, maybe?

"You woke me up about five minutes ago. You were tossing and turning and you clobbered me on the back. You were also moaning and panting like you were having the best sex of your life!"

As Peter's words sank in, Karen suddenly became aware of the ache between her legs and the decidedly damp sensation in her crotch. She gasped, and the dream came back to her. God, that would explain her unconscious behaviour and the fact she'd woken up feeling as horny as fuck, then. She'd had a seriously sexy dream. Practically pornographic, actually.

She'd been... she gasped again as she remembered. Bloody hell—she'd been shagging two men at once! Thankfully, one of them had been Peter, so she didn't have to lie to boost his ego. But the other man in her dream was a total surprise. It was Gabriel, Peter's best friend. She didn't even like the arrogant bastard, so it came as a total shock to her to discover that she'd dreamt about sleeping with him.

"Well?" Peter said, interrupting her reverie, his expression expectant. "Are you going to share with the class?"

"All right," she replied with a frown, "no need to get shirty with me. I can't help what I dream about, can I? Though you're right, I was having some seriously fantastic sex."

"Were you now?" His expression turned lecherous. "Pray, tell."

"You might not like it."

"What's that supposed to mean? That I wasn't involved? Okay, come on. Who was it? George Clooney? David Beckham?"

"Ugh, no! Not David Beckham. Though I certainly wouldn't say no to George." She paused. "Actually, you were involved."

"So why won't I like it, then? What's not to like about me and you having brilliant sex?"

Karen figured the sooner she got the words out, the sooner the two of them could have a blazing row and get it over and done with. She was beginning to wish she'd kept her mouth shut. Or lied.

"You probably won't like it because it wasn't *just* you I was having sex with."

Peter's eyebrows shot up. "Oh, really? So who was the other person in our threesome? Or was it more than three?"

He looked genuinely curious now, and Karen realised that perhaps he wouldn't be mad about it, after all. About the threesome thing, anyway. She was pretty sure he'd kick off when he found out who the other man had been.

She shook her head. "No, it was just three. Me, you, and…" She had to force the word out, so horrified was she that she had to say it at all. "Gabriel."

Peter's eyebrows almost disappeared into his hairline. "*Gabriel*? But I thought you hated him? Oh God, it's not one of those things where people pretend to hate other people when they're actually madly in love with them? Fuck, you're not in love with my best mate, are you?" He ran a hand through his hair, and his expression was genuinely worried.

"Hell, no! I really and truly can't stand the prick. No one is more surprised than me that I dreamt about him at all, never mind in that way. Anyway, I thought you'd be mad."

"Mad about what? That you dreamt about having a threesome, or that it was with Gabriel?"

"Both."

"No, why would I be mad about that? People can't control their dreams. God, if I could, I'd make myself dream about hot ménages every damn night. So, am I to take it that you mean you'd actually *like* a threesome in real life? With Gabriel?"

"Not with Gabriel. But with someone I actually like. That'd be pretty hot."

"Oh." Peter looked disappointed.

"What? I thought you'd be happy that I'm not secretly holding a torch for your best friend."

"No. I mean yes, I'm glad you're not in love with him. But I wouldn't mind if you shagged him—with me present, of course. You wouldn't be the first girl we've shared."

Now it was Karen's turn to raise her eyebrows. "Seriously? The two of you have shagged the same woman? At the same time?

Why didn't you tell me?"

Peter laughed. "Well, it's not exactly the sort of thing you tell a girlfriend, is it? 'Meet my best friend Gabriel. We've had threesomes with girls before, so if you're up for it, we are.' I don't think it'd go down too well, do you? But now you've expressed an interest…"

"In threesomes, not in him. Let's give it some thought, eh? See if we think it's something we're interested in. And if so, who with."

"Sounds like a plan to me."

Chapter Two

Over the next few days, though, Karen didn't need to make herself think about it. It seemed her brain could barely concentrate on anything else. Flashes of the dream came back to her on a regular basis—having two pairs of hands roaming her eager body, two mouths kissing her, nibbling her, licking her. Best of all, two cocks for her to lick, suck and fuck. It was no wonder her unconscious imaginings had left her so flustered—that dream shag really had been the best sex of her life. It wasn't that Peter wasn't good in bed—for all his faults, he *really* was—but having two men would be double the pleasure. Providing they were both skilled lays, that was. And, as much as she hated herself for even thinking it, she believed that Gabriel was indeed, a fantastic fuck.

All the times she'd been forced to socialise with Gabriel, he'd always had a companion. She said companion because none of them seemed to be around long enough to be classed as a girlfriend. Whatever they were, though, they were always deliriously happy. If Karen ever ended up alone with one of Gabriel's victims and the chat turned to their respective men, they always had nothing but good things to say about him. He was charming, fun to be with, a good kisser, and phenomenal in the bedroom. Of course they totally turned all that information on its head when they were invariably ditched by the not-at-all angelic man in question. She'd overheard the insulting telephone calls and seen the vile text messages, calling him all the unpleasant names under the sun. Hell hath no fury and all that.

The information about Gabriel's sexual prowess that Karen had been given, though, could not be unlearned. And it was this knowledge that seeped into her thoughts on a regular basis and made her think that perhaps it wouldn't be such a terrible thing to have a threesome with him and Peter, after all. She didn't have to talk to the bloke, or go on a date with him or anything like that. They'd just set it up so it was a very straightforward wham, bam, thank you ma'am type thing. But much more erotic and orgasm-worthy.

The more she thought about it, the more she figured that was definitely the way to go. If Peter and Gabriel had shared a woman before and Peter was happy to do it again, then it had obviously worked out okay. So why not have a smoking hot ménage a trois and get it out of her system once and for all? Maybe then she'd stop thinking about how Gabriel's body would feel pressed against hers, his cock buried deep inside her pussy. He may be a complete and utter arsehole, but he was also as sexy as fuck. And now she'd screwed him senseless in the land of nod, it didn't seem so much of a huge step to do it for real.

After another week, she couldn't keep her mouth shut any longer. She simply had to say something to Peter, otherwise she'd explode. To get him in the right sort of mood, she cooked him a lovely dinner and plied him with a glass or two of wine before bringing up the subject.

"So," she said, smiling broadly, though not so much that he might think she wasn't being serious, "you remember the conversation we had last week. About threesomes?"

A tiny frown line appeared between Peter's eyebrows, then disappeared. "Yes, of course. Why, have you given it some more thought?"

Are you kidding? I've barely been able to think about anything else.

"Actually, I have. And I was thinking that if you're still up for it, we could maybe ask Gabriel if he wants to be involved. Since you two have shared women before and your friendship is intact, then it obviously worked out okay. And because as a person I think the man is vile, there's no risk to our relationship either, is there? The three of us will just have a jolly lovely time in the sack, and that will be the end of it."

She sucked in a breath, and waited for her boyfriend to respond. Given his eyebrows had crept closer to his hairline with every word she'd spoken, she had no idea what he was going to say. Her fingers gripped her wine glass so hard it was in danger of shattering. She put it down.

"Okaaay," Peter said, his expression one of intense concentration. He closed his eyes for a second or two, then opened them again. "I must admit I suspected this conversation would happen at some point, but I didn't expect you to want Gabriel."

"Oh!" Karen replied. "I don't *want* him. Not like that. Well, I suppose I do, like *that.* But not in any other way. You know how I feel about him."

"Yes, I do. That's why I'm so surprised. But you've obviously thought about this and decided it would work for you, so if that's what you want, I'll sort it."

"Okay." Well, that had gone more smoothly than she'd expected. She'd known he wouldn't be mad about it, but she hadn't been entirely sure what kind of emotions her request would elicit. Surprise and then acceptance were absolutely fine by her.

Of course, that meant it would actually happen. A threesome between her, Peter and Gabriel. And, she realised as Peter fished his mobile phone from his pocket, it would happen very soon.

Chapter Three

As the water cascaded from the shower head onto her skin, Karen seriously considered hopping out, locking the bathroom door and not coming out until the next day. Maybe then Peter and Gabriel would forget about the whole thing. Forget she'd said anything. That she'd ever suggested a threesome with them. For fuck's sake. What had she been thinking? A ménage was way hot, but with Gabriel? What the actual fuck? She must have been crazy to suggest it.

She resisted the temptation to bang her head against the tiled wall. That would achieve nothing, except giving her a headache, and possibly a bruise. Instead, she stuffed her fingers into her mouth and hoped that and the noise of the shower would stifle her scream.

Ahh, that's better. Now the initial frustration and irritation were out of her system, perhaps she could apply her brain cells to finding a way of getting out of this.

She heard a muffled sound. Moving her head out from under the thundering spray, she listened. It came again. Someone was banging on the door. Ugh, typical Peter. He always wanted to use the toilet when she was having a shower. It was like he purposely waited until she was in there before deciding he needed to answer the call of nature.

"Karen! Have you drowned in there or something? Hurry up, he'll be here soon."

"What are you talking about? I haven't been in here that long!"

"You have, babe. You've been in there forty five minutes."

Fuck!

"Fuck! Okay, I'll be as fast as I can."

She rubbed her face. God, had she really been in here that long? Normally a shower took her twenty five minutes at most, and that included shaving her legs, underarms and between her legs. What the hell had she been doing for forty five minutes?

Looking down, she realised that she had, in fact, shaved all the usual places, and a scrape of fingers through her hair told her that conditioner had been applied. She could only assume that she'd used shampoo previous to that. She'd been so deep inside her own tortured mind that all she could do was assume, and she didn't have time to start everything all over again just to be sure. So with a thorough rinse, she turned off the shower, stepped out and pulled on her robe, tying it tight. Grabbing a towel, she wrapped up her hair to stop it dripping everywhere.

Heading out onto the landing, she shouted to Peter that she was out of the bathroom, just in case he did need the toilet. There was no response. She repeated herself. Still nothing.

"For fuck's sake." She stomped down the stairs, ready to give Peter a piece of her mind, and book him an appointment with a hearing specialist. That would soon sort out his selective hearing, if she threatened to send him to a professional. She barrelled into the living room.

"Are you deaf or some..." The words died on her lips as her brain caught up with her eyes. Gabriel was in her living room. Already. She hadn't seen him since she'd had the dream about him, and now, being presented with her illicit nocturnal fantasy in the flesh rendered her speechless. Even more so as she noted the way he was looking at her. Like a lion, and she was a deer, or some other kind of vulnerable prey. Except, of course, he wanted to fuck her, not eat her. She presumed.

Both men were staring at her. Silently, which somehow made it all the more nerve-wracking. If someone would just say something, perhaps that would alleviate the tension that suddenly filled the room so completely that she worried the patio doors would shatter under the strain.

"Umm..."

Gabriel stood up, aborting her attempt at speech. Even several paces away, he seemed to loom over her, his big body blocking what was behind him, which included Peter. Therefore she had no idea how her boyfriend was reacting as his best friend advanced on her, then stood before her, and, with a leering grin, said, "Are you ready for us, babe? Or are you getting cold feet?"

His expression softened slightly with his second sentence, and Karen realised that, for all his faults, Gabriel would not force her into anything she didn't want to do. Feeling slightly more comfortable in the knowledge, she relaxed and forced herself to look up at him. Tipping her head back until she could look into his cheeky green eyes, she felt a sudden jolt of arousal burn through her body.

Who was she kidding? There was no way she'd turn back now. Especially as she'd thought about little else for several days before getting Peter to set it up. If she chickened out now, she'd never forgive herself. She'd much rather regret something she'd done, rather than live out the rest of her days wishing she'd done it. If it didn't live up to expectations, well, then she'd stop fantasising and dreaming about it then, wouldn't she? So it was a win-win situation.

"No," she replied, her voice breathy as a result of the rapidly growing heat between her thighs, "I'm not getting cold feet. Far from it, in fact. But if you'll just give me a few minutes to get myself sorted out. I didn't realise I'd been in the bathroom for so long." She indicated her dressing gown and the towel on her head.

"Oh no," Gabriel said, "I think you're absolutely fine as you are. In fact, it's a lot easier to get you naked when you're like this, isn't it?"

He reached for the towel and gently pulled it from her hair, dropping it to the floor. Karen's heart pounded so hard and so fast she thought it would leap right out of her chest. His hands gripped the belt around her waist, but she grabbed his wrists and shot a panicky look towards the window that faced out onto the street.

"Wait," she said, gently pushing him away. "We can do this, I *want* to do this, but I don't want an audience peering in through my front window."

Gabriel let out a belly laugh. "Fair enough, babe. I understand. So, should I close the curtains?"

Karen sighed. She had to do something to stop the man talking, and soon. If he said much more stupid shit, she'd go off the idea of fucking him pretty rapidly.

"No, we'll go upstairs. There's more room and it'll be more comfortable."

With that, she turned and made her way out of the room before he could respond. But she wasn't quite fast enough and she still heard his comment, which was probably more aimed at Peter than her.

"Comfort isn't the first thing on my list of priorities, but hey, whatever the lady wants."

Chapter Four

As soon as she was out of sight of the living room, Karen scampered up the stairs and into the bedroom. As time had gotten away from her, not only had she not had chance to get dressed, put makeup on or do her hair, she also hadn't tidied up. She and Peter weren't massively untidy creatures, but at the end of a busy week there was often a pair of dirty socks or underwear lying around, or a damp towel. It was more down to lack of time than laziness. And right now, Karen was desperately trying to make up for lost time. She scooped up the few articles of soiled clothing on the floor and shoved them into the laundry basket. Then she kicked herself that she hadn't had the foresight to change the bed. But there was absolutely no time for that now, and she figured it didn't matter all that much, anyway. The three of them would be *on* the bed, not in it. And there was no way Gabriel was staying over—it was a fuck, not the beginning of a beautiful relationship.

Soon enough, she heard the sound of two sets of footsteps coming up the stairs. Quickly, she moved to her dressing table, retrieved her hairbrush and started tugging it through her hair at an alarming rate. She was minus more than a few strands of hair and sporting watery eyes by the time Peter and Gabriel entered the room, barefooted and grinning.

Taking a deep breath, she summoned up as much confidence as she could find inside herself. It wasn't much, but it was just enough to allow her to smile back at the men and to make a request. "You going to get your clothes off then, gentlemen?"

Ever the arrogant bastard, Gabriel shot back, "I will if you will, darlin'."

God, shut up, you prick! Stop fucking talking! Forcing the smile to stay on her face, she replied, "All I'm wearing is a dressing gown. It'll take me considerably less time to get naked than it will you two. So get on with it." She glared, and it seemed that the boys decided to do as they were told, rather than risking her wrath and the potential termination of their kinky plan.

Given they'd already removed their shoes and socks—a good plan, which meant they'd avoid the awkward and ungainly hopping around phase of undressing—mere seconds rendered them shirtless, and Karen watched in appreciative silence as the two extremely attractive men undid their jeans, let them fall to the floor and stepped out of them. She was a little surprised that Gabriel was wearing underwear, she'd had him pegged as the kind of guy that liked to go commando. However, the tight boxers did little to hide the erection that was already straining against them. A glance across at Peter told her that he was in much the same state.

"Okay," she said, the power she realised she had over them suddenly going to her head, "now the boxers."

Gabriel opened his mouth to say something, but she raised her eyebrows and gave him a pointed look. He got the hint, and then the two men complied with her wishes.

"Very good. Now get on the bed—Peter, if you could grab some condoms first—and then I shall join you."

They scrambled up onto the bed, then Peter reached into the top drawer of his bedside unit and grabbed a couple of condoms, passing one to his friend. They exchanged a look that could only be described as excited, then turned back to watch Karen untie the belt of her dressing gown, then shrug out of it.

Her pussy had started to become wet back in the living room, when Gabriel had first approached her. She'd grown steadily more aroused as their encounter progressed, and now, as she took in the two eager men sitting on her bed with stiff, delicious-looking cocks, a powerful zing of lust coursed through her body, centring in on her groin and leaving it hot and heavy. A gush of juices soaked her thighs. God, she was really going to do this, and she could only hope it was as hot and satisfying as her dream had been.

She got onto the bed, eyeing each man in turn and wondering where the hell to start. They'd done this before; she hadn't. She glanced at Peter to make sure he was still okay with everything. His nod, and the erection that pointed at the ceiling reassured her that he was. Then, figuring the best way to keep Gabriel quiet was to make sure his mouth was occupied, so she quickly straddled him. Settling into his lap, with his hard on pressing against her buttocks, she kissed him. He seemed a little startled at first—possibly at her sudden forwardness—but quickly relaxed into the embrace, slipping his arms around her back and pulling her closer, so her breasts pressed against his chest.

Now things had started, there was no hesitation. Karen quickly became a slave to her lust and forgot all about how much she despised the man she was currently kissing and let her libido guide her. The kiss deepened, grew more frenzied until finally she pulled away with a gasp, aware of how she was soaking Gabriel's thighs with her pussy juices. He grinned wolfishly at her, and before he could speak, she held a finger to his lips.

"Don't talk," she whispered. "Just fuck."

He shrugged, but kept quiet. With that, she shifted off of Gabriel and moved over to Peter. While she'd been kissing his friend, her mind had raced through the erotic possibilities of what lay ahead, and she'd made a decision. She definitely wanted them both inside her at the same time, and Peter was going to be in her cunt, Gabriel her arse. It wasn't down to cock size—she'd surreptitiously compared them, and they were pretty much the same—she knew that much, but she wasn't entirely sure why she'd made that decision. She suspected, though, that it was something to do with facing someone she actually liked. She could kiss and stroke Peter as they fucked, and she could almost imagine that Gabriel was someone else, or just a dick up her arse.

Taking the condom from Peter, she opened it, threw the wrapper on the floor and rolled the latex down his shaft. A sound from beside her hinted that Gabriel was doing the same thing. Pushing Peter back onto the pillows, she shuffled into position and lowered herself onto his cock. She let out a hiss as the thick, pulsing shaft stretched her, but she was so wet that it was a pleasurable, filling kind of stretch, rather than a painful one. She quickly grew used to the invasion and leaned down to give her boyfriend a long, passionate kiss which made her toes curl before sitting back up, ready to fuck.

Resting her hands on Peter's pecs, she braced herself against him as she began to rock her hips slowly, teasing them both as his cock slipped in and out of her. Once she gained the optimum rhythm, she turned to look at Gabriel. He was stroking his shaft slowly, closely watching the point of entry between her and Peter's bodies.

"Go into the top drawer there," she pointed to the cabinet on her side of the bed, "and get the bottle of lube. Then smother some all over that cock of yours and I'll let you know when I'm ready."

He said nothing—mercifully—and she turned her attention back to riding the man beneath her. She heard the telltale sounds of lube being squeezed from a bottle, and a thrill went through her at the thought of being completely full of cock—one in each hole. Well, except for her mouth, of course, but that was okay.

Soon, she was as hot and horny as it was possible to get

before coming, so she spoke over her shoulder. "Okay, lube me up, and don't be stingy with it, either."

"Yes ma'am."

She raised her eyebrows at his acquiescence, but figured that no man would cock block himself by being rude to the woman he was about to fuck. Not even one as stupid as Gabriel. She slowed her movements right down, then eventually stopped, lifting her arse up as high as she could without Peter's dick slipping out of her, so Gabriel could lubricate her rear hole.

He wasted no time, slicking copious amount of the chilly liquid around and around the tight pucker, before tentatively venturing a finger inside, making sure she was good and ready for him. He was patient and thorough—something she hadn't expected—and by the time she felt the bed shift as he moved up behind her, she was desperate to have him inside her. She closed her eyes as Gabriel moved into position. He stroked her arse cheeks and nudged the blunt head of his cock against her back entrance. She waited.

After a beat, she felt the bump of knuckles against her bottom as Gabriel gripped his shaft and aimed it carefully. Then she pulled in a deep breath through her nostrils, fighting hard to stay relaxed as he began to push inside her. He'd done a damn fine job of lubricating them both, so it didn't hurt exactly, but there was still a fair bit of resistance. Karen pushed against it, knowing that once he was seated inside her she'd quickly grow used to his size. She was no anal virgin—just a virgin to having both her holes filled at once.

Gritting her teeth, she dug her nails into Peter's chest, eliciting a gasp from him as her channels stretched and stretched. Eventually, Gabriel's body was pressed against hers. Nobody moved. She'd never felt so full in her life, and actually, it was every bit as arousing as she thought it would be—and they hadn't even gotten going yet. She waited a minute more before speaking. "Okay, boys. Do your worst. Not literally, though."

There were chuckles, and she kept her eyes closed, focussing on the pleasure as the two men worked together to get into a rhythm that was pleasurable for them all, and didn't dislodge one of their cocks. As they moved together, she was suddenly very aware that she could feel their shafts rubbing against one another through her thin internal walls. It was quite possibly the single most erotic sensation she'd ever experienced. She angled her hips so her clit was resting against Peter's pubic bone and hung on tight for the ride of her life.

And the ride of her life was definitely, one hundred and ten per cent, what she got. Once the men were satisfied she was okay, they picked up their pace, pumping in and out of her faster and harder until the white spots behind her eyes swirled and danced so wildly that she thought she was going to pass out. The pleasure was immense, immeasurable and indescribable. So when she felt her abdomen tighten, signalling the onset of an orgasm, she wasn't at all surprised. She just stayed as she was, allowing the ministrations of Peter and Gabriel to carry her swiftly along to a climax that left her screaming until her throat burned, causing Gabriel to clap a hand over her mouth.

"As fucking sexy as that is, Karen, if you keep that up the neighbours will think someone's murdering you and call the police."

She shook her head, trying to dislodge his hand. Eventually she succeeded, and she said, "All right, all right. Now shut up and fuck me until you both come."

The men needed no more persuading, and Karen tangled her fingers into the duvet and gripped it until her hands ached. Still they pounded into her. She was so wet that the room was filled with a rude wet clicking sound, but she didn't care. All she was really bothered about was reaching a second orgasm before Peter and Gabriel reached theirs. She suspected it wasn't far away—she felt as though every nerve ending was on fire, a delicious, all-consuming fire that made every touch, every caress threaten to burn her up.

She forced her hips downwards, grinding her pubic bone against Peter's hard, almost to the extent of pain. But she quickly forgot about that when the spark was ignited and she felt as though her entire body was alight with pleasure. The waves crashed through her body again and again and soon her moans were echoed by those of Peter and Gabriel as her clenching and twitching insides meant they couldn't hold their climaxes back any more.

Expletives filled the room, and the two thick cocks leapt inside her as their balls emptied into the condoms. Slowly, she sunk down onto Peter's chest, slipping into unconsciousness as her over-stimulated body shut down. She was vaguely aware of Gabriel pulling out of her, and then Peter gently rolled her off him and helped her to get into the bed.

"Thanks, Gabriel," she murmured, pulling the duvet up over

her head. "You can see yourself out."

She had a niggling thought that she should probably be nicer to Gabriel. After all, that had indeed been the best sex of her life, even better than the dream. And if she wanted to do it again, then she needed him on the side.

Nah, she decided. *If he wants to do it enough, he won't give a shit if I'm nice to him or not. He seemed happy enough that time.*

With that, she slipped into the sleep of the exhausted, a satisfied smile on her face, and a delicious ache between her thighs.

On the Night Bus

Emerging from the crowd, Will boarded the bus, swiped his travel pass across the electronic reader and scuttled hurriedly up the stairs. Relieved to note he was the only person on the top deck, he emphasised his need to be alone even further by walking to the rear of the bus and settling into a corner of the back seat. He was as far away from the other passengers as he could possibly get – and that was the way he wanted it.

Normally, he'd be happy to slum it with the laughing, slurring, swaying drunks on the lower deck – talking rubbish with them until it was time for him to get off the bus. Normally, he was *one* of the laughing, slurring, swaying drunks. It was Saturday night – or Sunday morning, depending on which way you looked at it – after all.

But tonight was far from normal. The realisation had sobered Will up in the blink of an eye, and sent him home before he did something he'd live to regret. Possibly not straight away – but certainly at some point. Like when he woke up in a cell at the local police station.

Just as Will felt his blood begin to boil again and his hands involuntarily clenched into fists, his solitude was ruined by the arrival of a young couple. They were drunk, giggly, and so wrapped up in each other that they didn't notice Will glowering in the corner. They slumped down together a few rows of seats in front of him and immediately began kissing as though their lives depended on it.

Will's glower deepened into a positively evil expression – luckily for the young couple his looks couldn't kill, otherwise they'd have been stone dead in an instant. It was hardly surprising he was pissed off, though. He'd just found out that his girlfriend and his so-called best friend had been seeing each other behind his back, and now a sickeningly loved-up couple were sucking face right in front of him. He hardly needed a reminder of his new single status, least of all such a vivid one.

Sighing, Will reached into his pocket and pulled out his iPhone. He'd switched it onto airplane mode earlier so none of the text messages and phone calls he knew the traitorous two would be trying to make would come through. There was absolutely nothing they could say that would excuse their behaviour, so he saw no reason to talk to either of them. Ever again.

Will was just about to fire up a game to distract him from the unwanted display in front of him when a moan that could only be described as lusty made him look up at the couple again. It was obvious that they really had no idea that he was sitting there, because their ardent kissing had now progressed to heavy petting. The guy had manoeuvred his girl's top down so both her breasts were on display. He yanked down the cups of her bra and sucked a nipple into his mouth, while he squeezed and pinched at the other one with an eager hand.

The girl's head lolled back, and her eyes fluttered closed; she was clearly lost in bliss. Not so lost that she couldn't voice her enjoyment, however. As her lover teased and pleasured her luscious tits, a constant cacophony of moans, grunts and squeals came from her parted lips. It was a good job that the lower deck of the night bus was so damn noisy and busy, otherwise they'd have been caught in no time and probably kicked off.

Will was actually a little surprised that the driver hadn't shouted at them through his intercom. He knew that drivers had some kind of clever mirror system in their cab which meant they could see what was happening on the top deck of the bus, to prevent such lewd behaviour. The couple were obviously too drunk to consider anything like that, and Will could only imagine that the squeeze of bodies, ever-present danger of vomiting and resultant havoc on the bottom level of the bus was keeping the driver thoroughly occupied.

The more he thought about it, the more he decided he was glad that they hadn't been disturbed. They'd totally distracted him from his personal problems, and for that he was grateful. So, it would seem, was his cock. Slipping his mobile back into his pocket, Will then pressed the palm of his hand against his rapidly growing erection. It twitched beneath his touch, and he glanced up again to check that he remained unnoticed in his corner. He did. In fact, Will suspected that even if the bus crashed, the pair would continue with their increasingly steamy clinch.

Deciding to take a chance, he undid the fly of his jeans and pulled out his stiff cock. He pumped it slowly in his fist as he watched the couple. Will wondered how far they would go before coming to their senses, sobering up or reaching the bus stop they needed to disembark at. As luck would have it, his stop was where the bus terminated so he'd get to find out the answer to this question without running the risk of going past his house and having to trek back across town to get home.

Soon, Will stopped thinking and simply watched and wanked. The breast play had ceased, and, although he couldn't actually see what was happening, it was damn obvious that the girl was now giving her boyfriend a blowjob. Her blonde head was bobbing up and down, and it was the man's turn to grunt and moan as his cock was enveloped in a hot, wet and *very* willing mouth. Will tugged his own shaft more vigorously, wishing he was the one getting head.

The noises the guy was making increased in intensity, and the girl suddenly sat up – her lips slipping off his cock with a wet pop. She grinned at him, and said, "You can't come yet, I want to fuck you."

"Be my guest." The guy's response was clearly all the invitation she needed. Some shuffling around ensued, and Will was suddenly terrified that the game was up as the girl straddled her man's lap, meaning she was facing him – and, as a consequence, Will, too. All she had to do was look up, and she'd spot the guy in the corner, wanking over a free live sex show. He froze in place, as though staying still would make him somehow invisible.

Will couldn't believe his luck, however, as the woman alternated between being forehead-to-forehead with her lover as she bounced on his cock, and tossing her blonde mane around like a porn star, with her eyes tightly closed.

Feeling a little more secure now, Will relaxed and picked up the pace on his prick. He'd barely noticed the stop-start of the bus as it wound its way along the route, but he knew it couldn't be much longer before it was at its finishing point. And there was no way he wanted to be caught with his cock out – by the couple, or anyone else, for that matter.

He needn't have worried. The frantic screwing taking place in front of him, with the titillating view of the hot blonde bouncing up and down, her tits doing the same, meant that Will's climax was just around the corner. He paced himself, though, aiming to come when one of the couple did, therefore drowning out any sounds Will might let slip.

It wasn't long before he got his opportunity, and it didn't come a moment too soon. As the bus drew to its final stop, and the driver shouted "Everybody off!" the girl hit her peak, letting out a stream of expletives. Her boyfriend rapidly followed suit, as did Will. He bit his lip so hard he almost drew blood as jet after jet of cum flew out of his cock, coating the back of the seat in front of him, his hand and his dick.

However, the timing and the situation were as such that Will couldn't worry about all that. Instead, he tucked his softening cock back into his jeans, grimacing at the thought of his spunk smearing over the inside of the denim. With the lack of any other option, he ignored his conscience and wiped his right hand on the seat's upholstery, zipped up his fly, then stood up and walked down the aisle of the bus towards the stairs.

With a huge grin and a "good night" to the startled couple scrabbling to put their clothes back on, Will descended the stairs, hopped off the bus and headed for home, hoping they wouldn't follow him and demand an explanation.

As he meandered his way home, Will suspected that despite the shitty night he'd had, he would have no trouble sleeping. The mind-blowing climax he'd just had would see to that.

It had brought a whole new meaning to getting off at his stop.

Naughty Delivery

Sonia moved restlessly through the house, cleaning. She hated housework at the best of times, but when she was on tenterhooks like this, the dust certainly didn't have much to fear.

She was saved from her half-hearted duster-flicking by a knock at the door. Abandoning the cloth with undisguised glee, Sonia rushed to the front door. Unlocking it, she greeted the delivery guy with a maniacal grin. Barely noticing his wary expression, Sonia signed his hand-held machine and closed the door behind him, clutching the box with delight.

Sonia rushed out to the garden.

"Ben! Ben, it's here!"

Ben looked up from where he'd been weeding the garden, a smile spreading across his handsome face. Sonia's excitement was catching. Plus, he was just as interested in the contents of the package as she was.

Standing, he followed his girlfriend as she scampered back into the house, retrieved a pair of scissors from the kitchen drawer and made her way upstairs. Ben paused to wash his dirt-encrusted hands in the kitchen before heading to the bedroom.

Upstairs, she was sitting cross-legged on their bed, scissors at the ready. Ben tucked his lanky frame into a mirror image of Sonia's position, and nodded.

"Go on then," he said, "open it."

She didn't need prompting twice. Slicing away at the tape sealing the box, Sonia was careful not to damage the contents. When it was done, she put the scissors down and waggled her eyebrows and fingers theatrically before folding back the flaps of the box.

Sinking her fingers into the polystyrene packing chips, Sonia resisted the childish temptation to scoop some up and throw them around. She'd only have to tidy them up; and she thought that time would be much better spent enjoying the contents of the parcel.

It was the first time they'd ordered sex toys from the internet. Actually, it was the first time they'd purchased any sex toys, full stop. Ben and Sonia had always been happy with their sex life, but after reading one too many articles about how much fun vibrators and things were, they'd decided to find out what all the fuss was about.

They'd giggled like naughty schoolchildren as they scoured their website of choice, browsing through all the sexy things available for sale. After gawping wide-eyed and open-mouthed at several scary-looking implements definitely *not* designed for beginners, they'd navigated back to the more vanilla couples' toys.

Following some umm-ing and ahh-ing, they made their choices, placed the order and waited. However, things weren't quite the same after they'd clicked that 'Confirm Purchase' button. In the days that followed, their normal routine was punctuated with spontaneous sex. It usually followed a conversation about the various things they'd seen on the website, not to mention the items that were winging their way through the postal system, en route to their house.

Or so they thought.

Ben looked on with anticipation as Sonia's hands delved into the box. He watched her expression change as she touched something other than polystyrene; her eyes lighting up. His cock twitched as his mind raced ahead, considering the possibilities of what was about to happen.

When Sonia brought a leather spanking paddle out of the package, the silence was palpable. She looked at Ben, a crease appearing between her eyebrows. Tossing the implement onto the bed, Sonia continued to rummage around in the box. The items she brought out in her hands next shouldn't have been surprising, considering the spanker. But they were.

Because Sonia and Ben had *not* ordered thick leather wrist and ankle cuffs to go with the paddle. They hadn't even ordered the paddle. Ben reached over to take the heavy cuffs from Sonia and lay them down next to the spanker.

Sonia soon unearthed the packing slip from the bottom of the box. Eyes flicking down the page, the crease between her eyebrows grew deeper.

"This is really weird," she said, passing a hand across her forehead, as if to erase the confusion. "Something's gone completely wrong here. This slip is actually correct."

"Look," she continued, turning the sheet of paper so Ben could read it, "it's got the right name, address, items and price. But the wrong items have been packed. They've obviously fucked up in their warehouse. Someone is sitting at home like we are now, expecting all this kinky shit, and they've got our stuff!"

"Well," said Ben, looking across to where the offending items lay. "There's not a lot we can do about it right now, is there?"

"Not really." She sighed. "I'm pretty pissed off though. I was in the mood for a bit of fun."

A glint in his eye, Ben grasped the handle of the spanker. Turning his gaze to Sonia, he said, "What do you mean, 'was?' What's to stop us from having some fun anyway?"

He brought the flat of the paddle down hard on his palm, grinning wolfishly as Sonia yelped at the sound.

"You want to use that stuff?" Sonia said, looking worriedly at the heavy-duty cuffs.

"Well, it seems a shame to waste it. And you've always said you'd try anything once."

"Within reason, I said!"

"Come on," Ben chided, "it's only a bit of bondage, a bit of spanking. Let's give it a go. I'll tie you up first, then maybe later we can reverse roles. If we're not into it, we'll stop. It's no biggie."

Sonia looked at Ben, who copied her eyebrow-wiggling of earlier. She shrugged. "Why not? I guess we'll never know if we don't try."

"That's my girl. Now get your kit off and let me see that gorgeous body of yours."

Sonia shifted off the bed, moving the box, complete with its polystyrene contents onto the floor. She kicked off her shoes, then bent to pull off her socks. Standing, she started unbuttoning her blouse.

The pace obviously wasn't quick enough for Ben, who yelled, "Quicker than that, come on!"

Sonia looked wide-eyed at her boyfriend and considered teasing him all the more for his impatience. That would have been her usual reaction. But when he started tapping the paddle against his palm, she decided against it. He was obviously getting into character; he'd gone all masterful, getting off the bed and stretching to his full height, so he towered over her, glowering.

Sonia was surprised to discover that, far from finding Ben's sudden dominance ridiculous or amusing, it was making her hot. They'd always been equals in the bedroom, but now the thought of being taken and ravished by Ben was causing a delicious heat in her groin that was only going to get hotter.

Shedding her clothes as quickly as she could, Sonia soon

stood naked before Ben. Without realising it, she'd also slipped into character, standing there silently and awaiting her next orders.

"Good," said Ben, still tapping the paddle against his hand, "now get onto the bed, and spread 'em."

As Sonia turned to do Ben's bidding, he aimed a sharp smack at her rounded bottom, causing her to squeal and leap onto the bed. She spread-eagled herself quickly before any more spanks could be laid on her arse. As she watched for Ben's next move, she felt the skin he'd struck grow warm and tingly. It wasn't an unpleasant sensation, but Sonia suspected there hadn't been much force behind the blow. Nevertheless, her pussy grew warmer at the thought of more force being applied.

Ben, still fully dressed, climbed onto the bed and picked up the wrist restraints. Shuffling up towards Sonia's head, he knelt by her side, examining the cuffs to see how they worked. Soon, he slipped Sonia's hand inside the faux-fur lined leather and did up the fastenings.

Breaking out of character briefly, he said, "Any time you're not happy or comfortable, you let me know. I suppose we should have a safe word. That's what they do, right?"

Sonia nodded.

"Okay," he continued, "the safe word is 'bananas'. You say that, we stop. Okay?"

Sonia nodded again, and Ben dropped a kiss on her head. "Good girl. Now put your arms above your head so I can chain you to the bed."

She did as she was told. Ben slipped one of the slim chains around a bar at the head of the bed and clipped it to the first cuff. Then, reaching over her, he secured Sonia's other wrist and attached the chain. She was now officially tied up. Of course, that was only half the game.

Moving down her body, Ben repeated the process with Sonia's ankles. Once he'd finished, he got off the bed and moved across the room, turning to study his handiwork from a distance. He'd had a semi-on ever since Sonia had started undressing, and it had taken some real determination to keep his head as he trussed her up.

Now, though, looking at his girlfriend all tied up and presented to him like a gift, Ben's cock thickened. It pushed against the material of his boxers and jeans, eager to be let out. Sonia looked stunning. Her colour was high, her eyes shone and even from here he could see that her pussy was glistening with juices. He couldn't wait to play with and tease her until she begged him to fuck her.

Ben stripped without preamble, leaving his clothes in a pile on the floor and walked back to where Sonia waited. He joined her on the bed and moved into a kneeling position between her spread legs. Retrieving the spanking paddle, he held it up.

Looking into Sonia's eyes, he spoke. "You look so delicious, I barely know where to start."

Sonia said nothing, jiggling a little as if to test her bonds. Her breasts bobbed and bounced, drawing Ben's attention. "Or perhaps I do."

As the paddle impacted on Sonia's pale flesh, she yelped. Ben knew it was just impulse; he was just testing the waters and hadn't so far struck her very hard at all. Besides, although she'd made a noise, she hadn't struggled or protested. He aimed a whack on the other breast.

Sonia squeaked again, then lay still, body tense and aching with anticipation. Ben wasn't striking her very hard, but she suspected he was sussing out her pain threshold. She trusted him implicitly and knew he would never hurt her. Not any more than she wanted him to, at least.

The thought startled her, but really she shouldn't have been surprised. Her brain may not have caught up, but her body was certainly reacting to the punishment Ben had been meting out. She could feel the heat in her cheeks and cunt, and her nipples were hard little nubs, sticking up like buoys from a sea of reddened flesh.

Ben increased the pace and force of his strokes until Sonia felt like she was on fire. She moaned and gasped as the sensation overwhelmed her, her pussy seeping juices down her crack and onto the bed sheets. Each blow was like a firework going off; the initial bang, a delay, then the slow spread of little dots and streaks of light.

When Ben stopped what he was doing, Sonia's eyes flew open. She hadn't fully realised they'd been closed. She watched as he shifted position, moving lower on the bed.

From his new vantage point, Ben had the most perfect and delicious view of Sonia's pussy. It was spread before him, soaking wet and silently begging to be fucked. He wanted to. Oh God, did he want to. However, he also wanted to see how much further he could push Sonia's limits. She'd come easily if he fucked her now, he knew that. But he wanted to see if some of the rumours were true; that the longer he held off, the more explosive her eventual climax would be.

His cock throbbed painfully as he thought about Sonia's tight cunt and what it felt like to be inside it. He'd be there, soon enough. But first…

Sonia jumped as the first blow landed on her inner thigh. Ben had been studying her pussy so intently that she'd closed her eyes, silently praying that his resolve would crack and that he'd stuff his cock inside her and fuck her until they both came. Obviously that was not going to happen. Yet.

The pale skin of her inner thighs quickly changed colour as Ben alternated strokes on each. He was careful not to hit the same spot too many times, and soon Sonia's flesh was pink and red from crotch to knee. She was so high on the sensation that she felt like she would come if Ben so much as blew on her clit. Oh, if only he would do something. The tiny cluster of nerve endings was distended and aching. Sonia desperately wanted to climax, but it was not up to her.

Ben was in charge. She was helpless and she loved it. Somehow, removing her freedom of choice had freed her. She was completely at her lover's mercy; didn't have to think or do anything. Just feel what was being done to her by the man she loved.

And right now, he was discarding the spanking paddle and covering her with his big body. He leaned down to kiss her lips and as she opened her mouth to admit his tongue, he thrust his cock inside her soaked pussy.

As soon as Ben's pubic bone rubbed against her tortured clit, she came. And came.

When it was over, she decided she was mighty glad the sex toy company had screwed up the order. She had no idea what sex would have been like with the cock ring and mini-vibe they'd actually ordered, but right then, she didn't care.

She was so satiated that she had half a mind to write them a letter of thanks.

Dear sex toy company. Thanks for fucking up our order and the mind blowing orgasms that resulted.

Sonia giggled, making Ben stir in her arms. She quieted, not wanting to wake him up. Her gaze fell on the abandoned box on the floor. She smiled.

Thanks indeed.

The Only Bitch For Me

It had been so long since I'd seen her that I'd almost forgotten how bossy she could be. She sauntered up – late, as usual – to where I was standing at the bar. We greeted one another with a hug and a kiss on each cheek. Before I could utter a word she gave me a cursory once over and piped up, "Are you going to buy me a drink then?"

No niceties, not even a "how are you?" You wouldn't think I'd just returned from a fucking war zone, would you? Six months in Afghanistan, risking life and limb. Cool as a cucumber, she was. And yet at the same time, she was so hot she'd make Satan sweat.

However, I was used to Cassie and her ways by now. So without missing a beat, I asked what she wanted and gave her order to the barman. Taking the drinks, I followed her and her wiggling arse as she made her way to a table. When she selected one as far away from all the other patrons as possible, I knew how this was going to play out. My cock twitched in anticipation.

Placing the drinks down on the table, I hurried to pull out her chair and help her into it. She nodded her thanks and took a sip from her wine glass as she waited for me to sit down.

"So you're back then," she said, eyeing me, as if looking for scars or wounds. I had none. Others hadn't been so lucky.

"Um, yes." I said, confused. Of course I was back, was I not sitting right in front of her?

"I meant for good. Back for good, smart arse."

"Sorry. Yes. I'm back for good. I'm now officially a civilian."

"So that means no more taking orders without question, huh? You have your own free will to do what you want, when you want."

Before I could respond, I felt her foot slipping in between my legs. But this was no stocking-clad caress. She was still wearing her stilettos, and the pointed toe of one of them pushed against my cock, which had begun to swell within my underwear. I gulped.

"I guess not. Not in my professional life, anyway."

She raised an eyebrow.

The conversation was temporarily halted as a waiter came to the table, notepad and pen poised.

"Good evening," he said, smiling at us both and completely

oblivious to what was taking place under the table, "will you be eating with us this evening?"

I was about to ask him to come back in a few minutes when we'd had chance to peruse the menu. But Cassie clearly had other ideas. Pressing her toe painfully against my burgeoning erection, she replied, "No, thank you. But would you mind bringing us another bottle of this wine and charging it to Mr. Holden's room?" She pointed out the bottle in question on the menu.

Expensive tastes. But that was Cassie all over.

"Certainly, madam. I'll be right back."

Alone once more, I looked at her, waiting for an explanation. I didn't prompt her, knowing she'd only speak when she was good and ready.

Cassie's foot began moving, chafing up and down my crotch. It was both less and more painful than before; she was no longer digging the toe of her shoe into me, but she was making my cock so hard that I felt like it was going to burst out of my clothes, Incredible Hulk style. If she carried on much longer, I was going to come in my pants. She'd love that, humiliating me and making me sit there with my own spunk drying and cooling in my underwear. She'd get off on it.

"We're going to get room service." She finally deigned to tell me; her foot now alternating between rough strokes and sharp little digs. I gritted my teeth as I felt my balls tighten in anticipation of their release. "And then you're going to make me come. Depending on how well you do, I may possibly let you climax too. Then, and only then, will we have a conversation about our future."

As I felt my orgasm approach, I knew two things for certain. One; that I couldn't wait to bury my face between her legs and feel her come all over my face, and two; that whilst I was on my knees, I would beg Cassie to be my wife.

After all, she was the only bitch for me. And she knew it.

Belle and the Beasts

Belle walked up the long gravel driveway, begrudging every step that brought her closer to the looming property at its end. She'd deliberately left the mansion house until last, and even as she reached the gate she'd crossed her fingers that it would be locked so she could turn around and go home. No such luck. It swung open easily, and her potential excuse for not knocking on the front door disappeared into thin air.

She tried to convince herself that it wouldn't be that bad. Perhaps her sister, Anna, had been exaggerating when she said that the inhabitants were just as creepy and unpleasant as the house itself. Anna was known for her wild imagination, after all.

The thought steeled her resolve. Belle stood straighter, and increased her pace up the seemingly never-ending drive. Soon, she caught her first glimpse of the house between the trees that lined the path. *Ugh.* Anna hadn't been exaggerating about the building, at any rate. It was just as spooky as she'd described it. If a person was being polite, they'd call it gothic. If they were being honest, they'd call it a dump. It was all turrets, balconies and tiny, grubby-looking window panes. It had probably been gorgeous in its heyday, but now it just screamed neglect.

It didn't matter what she thought, anyway. She was just here to collect the confounded book and be on her way. Anna was really poorly in bed, and she'd begged Belle to go around the neighbourhood and do her catalogue collection so she didn't lose any time or potential orders. Being the caring, dutiful big sister, Belle had agreed. And now here she was, at the last house on the route and just one door knock away from heading back home to curl up with a good book.

Reaching the huge, imposing front door, adorned with a grotesque gargoyle-type thing, Belle rolled her eyes. It was like these people had gone out of their way to make their house as uninviting as possible to keep people away. What could possibly make them so anti-social? Surely they didn't just keep themselves to themselves, and never venture into the outside world. Who could live like that?

Pushing her thoughts aside, Belle grasped the gargoyle-knocker and rapped smartly on the door. She took a small step back and waited. And waited. Soon, she wondered if nobody was in, or if they were just ignoring the door. There was no way they didn't hear her knocking on the door. Unless they were showering, or in the garden, or listening to music...

She knocked again. Just one more catalogue to go and she could hand the lot over to her sister. Job done.

The door swung open, and immediately Belle saw why Anna was always so reticent about visiting this place.

"What?" said the man who now stood in the doorway, his arms folded. "What do you want?"

Belle, who was rarely lost for words, couldn't quite make hers come out properly. "I—I've come for th—the makeup catalogue."

"Oh, it's *you*, is it?" He peered at her, his expression impossible to fathom underneath so much hair – facial and regular. "Well, tell whoever is in charge to stop putting these damn things through the door. There are no women living here, so what do we want with bloody makeup?"

With that, he stepped back into the gloom of the hallway and retrieved something from a table. Holding it out to Belle, the man continued, "And the next time, it's going in the bin, all right? I'm fed up of them!"

Belle snatched the catalogue from his hand, indignant at the way she was being spoken to. "All right, all right. I'll pass the message on. There's no need to be so bloody *beastly,* is there? No wonder there are no women living here, if you speak to them like that!"

Then, before she had chance to turn tail and get the hell away from the nasty piece of work, his arm shot out and grabbed hers.

"Beastly?" he said, leaning in close and all but growling into her ear. "I'll show you beastly!"

With that, he tugged her into the house and slammed the door behind them, dragging her into the next room and pushing her into a chair. She dropped her bag of catalogues in the hall in her fright. Belle's already elevated pulse began to pound madly and she gripped the arms of the chair to try and alleviate her panic. What had she done? She'd stood up for herself against this man and had obviously sparked an awful temper. Now she had to get out of here as soon as possible. There was no telling what he was going to do.

Trying to outrun him was useless, she knew. He stood at least a foot taller than her, and despite his incredibly unkempt appearance—which, she couldn't help noticing, seemed to match the state of his house—he looked as though he cared for his physique.

That left trying to reason with him. Which, considering the way he'd flown off the handle wouldn't be an easy task, either.

Suddenly, Belle had a thought. When he'd been mid-rant, he'd said "we," with regards to the inhabitants of the house. So that meant there was someone else living there. Perhaps they'd be more reasonable than this hairy, grumpy so-and-so. She just had to figure out how to get them—no, *him,* there were no women living in the house—down here. Screaming would just antagonise her would-be abductor, and who knew if he'd turn violent? She wouldn't be any use to anyone with a broken neck, or a slit throat.

It was simple. She'd have to keep The Beast—as she'd started thinking of him—talking, and hope that the sound of their conversation would pique the curiosity of the other fellow and bring him down here to make his housemate see sense and let her go.

As The Beast paced up and down the wooden floor in front of her chair, Belle looked around, trying to figure out the layout of the house. It was huge, so there was no telling whether her plan would work. The other man could be in the furthest wing where even her loudest scream might not reach his ears. It didn't matter. She had to give it a shot, anyway.

In her loudest voice, Belle said, "What do you want with me? I'm sorry for what I said to you, but I just didn't appreciate being spoken to like that."

The Beast froze; then, without moving the rest of his body, turned his face towards her. The effect was eerie, and Belle squirmed in her chair.

In a low, menacing tone, he said, "I told you. I'm going to show you beastly."

Keeping her expression neutral, Belle had to concede to herself that she had no idea what he was talking about. Therefore she had no clue how to respond.

"Um, okay," she said. "Would you like to elaborate?"

He spun his entire body to face her this time, drawing up to his full height and looming over her as he barked the words, "Do you even know what you are saying, girl? You *want* to see beastly? You have no idea what you are asking for."

She hadn't been aware she'd been asking for anything, other than him to stop talking in riddles, but his words set the cogs in her brain turning. The way he kept repeating the word *beastly,* it was almost as if rather than using it as a describing word, he was using it as a name. *I'm going to show you Beastly.*

If she was right, then she was sure in trouble. Because if this guy—The Beast—had someone that *he* called Beastly, then she should at least try to make a run for it, rather than waiting to see who could possibly be worse. If she stayed here, she was a sitting duck, and she'd always thought if anything like this ever happened to her, she wouldn't go down without a fight. Of course, she'd never actually believed she'd end up in such a predicament. But hey, life was full of surprises.

Just as she tensed her arms, ready to propel herself out of the chair and make a bid for freedom, a noise drew both hers and The Beast's attention to the huge winding staircase to Belle's left. Hardly knowing what she was doing, Belle let out a hearty laugh.

"Him?" She slapped the arm of the chair in her mirth. "He's Beastly? You've got to be joking. He's—"

By now, the newcomer had descended the stairs, bypassed The Beast and drawn closer to her. When he stood right in front of her chair, he folded his arms, adopted a bored expression and said, "I'm what?"

Belle had to force the words out of her mouth, and when they came they were barely audible, even to her. "You're... *gorgeous.*"

It was true. This man—Beastly, apparently—was the most attractive man she'd ever laid eyes on. He had longish hair so dark it was almost black, and looked like he'd just tumbled out of bed. He was pale, with an aquiline nose, high cheekbones and blue eyes ringed by long dark lashes that she felt she could stare into forever.

She was making a start on the forever when a strangled sound came from The Beast. Belle snapped her attention from Beastly to The Beast—really, these names were getting quite confusing—wondering what on earth was wrong with him. It was only when he doubled over, clutching his stomach that she realised what was going on. He was laughing. At her.

He choked out some words in spite of his hilarity. "G— gorgeous? She thinks you're gorgeous, mate! Beastly's got an admirer!"

Beastly spun to face his housemate. Belle couldn't see his face, but she suspected he wasn't amused. His next words both confirmed her suspicions, and revealed the nature of their relationship.

"Shut up, brother. Or I will shut you up."

His tone was as cold as ice, and a shiver ran up Belle's spine, even though the words hadn't been directed at her. An inkling came to her of exactly why he might be called Beastly.

Belle watched as he turned ninety degrees. He could now see both her and his brother, whose mirth had disappeared and was replaced with a look of chagrin.

"So," he said, nodding his head towards Belle, "what is she doing here? I presume she's not your new girlfriend."

Now it was Beastly's turn to laugh, and although the relevant sound came from his lips, the emotion never reached his eyes.

He really was a cold, creepy motherfucker, Belle thought. And yet... as she looked at him—at both of the brothers, in fact—she experienced a tingling in her groin which was usually reserved for when she read dirty romance novels. What the hell was wrong with her? Surely she wasn't turned on by this situation? Two brothers, one super hairy with a vile temper, and the other who was perfection personified and yet as scary as fuck. They could have dozens of mutilated bodies buried in the extensive grounds of their crumbling mansion. Her thoughts were interrupted by The Beast's response.

"No, of course she's not my girlfriend. She's just some girl who came to collect that stupid makeup catalogue, and she pissed me off. I dragged her in here to teach her a lesson."

"And what exactly were you going to do? Beat her? Turn her into your personal sex slave?"

Belle gasped, then clapped both hands over her mouth, but of course it was too late. Her reaction had been noticed by both men, who were now staring openly at her. Their own conversation forgotten, there was silence for several uncomfortable seconds, before Beastly recovered. A sardonic smile crept onto his lips, and he rested one hand on his hip before speaking.

"I think..." he paused, clearly for effect, "that she likes that idea."

Belle didn't move a muscle. Couldn't. She didn't even deny Beastly's accusation. Her gaze flicked between the two men, and the heat grew in her groin as she thought about what it would mean to be their sex slave. Yes, *their*. She had no idea why, but she wanted both of them. In the wake of his brother's appearance, The Beast was still incredibly ugly, but much less terrifying. And if you discounted his chilling personality, Beastly was the stuff of female wet dreams everywhere. A tiny part of her mind relaxed as it realised that they wanted to have sex with her, not kill or maim her. Hopefully they didn't want to do all of the above.

Still wearing the sardonic smile, Beastly moved back towards where she sat, frozen, in the chair. He leaned down and placed his hands on top of hers, pinning her into place—not that she needed it.

"Am I right, little lady," he said, his beautiful face mere inches from hers, "in thinking that you'd like to be my brother's sex slave?"

Belle's face heated so extremely that she was surprised it didn't burst into flame. She gulped, and opened her mouth to respond. She managed nothing but a croak.

Beastly's grip on her hands increased. "Speak, then, girl! Do you want him, or..." He grinned, another thought clearly having popped into his head. "Perhaps you want both of us? Am I right?"

Belle tensed her thighs, the mere thought of going to bed with the two brutes sending her pussy into overdrive. The movement drew her attention to the wet heat already pooling between her legs. If only she could make herself speak, she was almost certain they'd give her what she so desperately wanted.

The incessant throbbing of her clit finally helped her to find her voice. Belle cleared her throat. "Yes. You're right. I want both of you. None of that slave crap, though. I just want a good, hard, fuck. With both of you."

Looking over his shoulder, Beastly said, "Hear that, brother? The girl wants a good hard fuck. With both of us. You up for that?" He turned back to Belle and continued talking without waiting for a response. "Of course he's up for that. He hasn't gotten laid since—"

"Beastly..." The Beast's tone was warning, and immediately Belle wanted to know what he'd been about to say.

However, it didn't look as though she was going to find out any time soon. Beastly's words had been cut off by his brother's interruption, and he didn't try to continue. Instead, he said, matter of factly, "Well, it seems we're all on the same page. Shall we retire to the master bedroom..." he held out a hand to Belle, and continued, "...actually, I have no idea what your name is. Decorum dictates that my brother and I should at least know your name before we take you to bed and have our wicked way with you."

He gave a sharp, sudden laugh, then widened his eyes, as

though waiting for her response. Belle shook herself before she got sucked back into gazing into his mesmerising eyes.

"S—sorry," she said, allowing Beastly to pull her into a standing position. "My name is Belle."

"Okay, Belle," said Beastly, leading her towards the staircase he'd descended earlier, "now we're all about to go upstairs to have 'a good hard fuck' as you so aptly put it. However, despite my nickname, I am not a total and utter shit, so if you want to change your mind, now's your last chance."

Belle wondered if he'd noticed how clammy her hand had become, clasped in his. She looked at each of the brothers in turn— one on either side of her—and a delicious frisson of arousal mixed with a tinge of fear zinged through her body before gathering in her groin. Straightening her back and holding his gaze with as much confidence as she could muster, Belle replied, "If you've got condoms, then I'm up for it."

Beastly gave a curt nod. "Come."

He led her up the stairs. The Beast stayed on her other side and Belle felt like she was a prisoner being escorted by guards. The thought gave her pause. *Was* she a prisoner? Her rational mind said no. After all, Beastly had given her a chance to back out of going to bed with the two of them, so surely he wouldn't force her into imprisonment, or worse.

Another thought came to her. If she was in danger, the longer she stalled the two men, the more likely it would be that her sister and father would come to look for her. They knew where she'd gone and approximately how long she'd be, so if she didn't return they would worry. If she just kept the brothers occupied in bed for as long as possible, then her family would turn up to escort her home safely.

Satisfied with her reasoning, Belle relaxed. From now on, she'd just go with the flow and see what happened. Peeking at each man in turn using her peripheral vision, she knew exactly what was going to happen. A multitude of fucking and orgasms, that's what.

Beastly reached a door on the first floor and twisted the handle. He pushed it open and ushered her in before him. Odd, that he should be so gentlemanly now, when he could be such a bastard, too. Perhaps he wanted to get laid as much as she did. Each step she'd taken up the stairs, along the landing and towards the huge four-poster bed in the master bedroom had emphasised the state of her underwear—incredibly damp and sticking to her skin.

Now she stopped and faced the two men who were standing just inside the room, watching her. Beastly wore a hungry expression, passion burning in his usually cool gaze. There was no telling with The Beast, but he was here, so he obviously wanted what everyone else wanted. As if reading her mind, he reached out a hand and pushed the door closed.

The sound snapped the three of them into action. Belle slipped off her shoes and tucked them under the edge of the bed. The Beast retrieved a hair tie which had been around his wrist and secured his mass of wild curls at the nape of his neck.

Beastly made the boldest move of all. Completely unabashed, he removed all of his clothes in record speed, moved to the bedside drawer and grabbed a handful of condoms, tossed them onto the duvet, then followed them.

Belle stared at the incredibly attractive man who now lay on the bed. He'd folded his arms behind his head, and crossed his legs at the ankles. His cock swelled rapidly, bobbing almost humorously from the dark curls at his groin. It was already very sizeable, and Belle's pussy moistened further at the thought of it being inside her. She turned to his brother, wondering if he'd been equally blessed.

The Beast still stood at the side of the room, and had made no further moves. Now Belle could see a little more of his face, she thought he looked... hesitant. He returned Belle's gaze, then shuffled back towards the door.

"Maybe I should—" he put a hand on the door handle.

"Don't you dare, brother. Belle said she wanted both of us, and both of us she shall have. Besides, it may be our only chance—"

Clearly eager to stop Beastly from saying any more, The Beast moved away from the door and advanced on Belle. Close up, he still looked as dishevelled as ever, but she also noticed how good he smelled. Soap, shampoo, and pure maleness. A glance down at his denim-covered crotch told her that he was aroused, too. He was definitely up for it, he just didn't have the confidence his brother did. But then he didn't have the looks, either. She guessed the two things went hand-in-hand.

"Hey," she said, grabbing her belt buckle. "I will if you will."

Even beneath the beard and moustache, there was no mistaking it—The Beast smiled. Belle returned the sentiment, and began undressing. He matched her garment for garment, but given she'd been dressed for the outdoors and also had a bra to contend with, he finished first. As she dropped her bra to the floor, she took the time to drink in the sight before her. Sure, he needed a haircut and a shave, but he had a body hot enough to rival his brother's. Not to mention his cock, which was rock hard and straining up towards his belly button.

She clenched her thighs together, already incredibly turned on by what she was about to do. It was just so taboo. Belle was no virgin—though if her father asked, of course she was—but she'd never been with two guys at the same time. The fact they were brothers just seemed to make it even more kinky.

She wondered if they'd shared a woman before. The way the situation had come together led her to believe that they had. Not that it really mattered. What mattered was her, now. And she'd been promised a good, hard fuck.

"Are you two just going to look at each other all day, or are you going to get over here so we can have some fun?" Beastly said, waving the condoms at the two of them. He moved over so he was closer to the edge of the bed, then patted the duvet next to him. "Come on, Belle. Get in the middle, and I promise you that my brother and I will show you a good time. One you'll never forget."

His words affected her as much as a tongue in her slit. She felt pussy juices trickling down her thighs, and her clit throbbed, desperate for attention. God, if she was this horny now, what was it going to be like when there were two pairs of hands on her; two mouths, and two cocks?

It was time to find out. Belle joined Beastly on the bed, with The Beast following close behind her. Sandwiched between them, Belle felt vulnerable yet powerful at the same time. Vulnerable because she was basking in the heat of two hulking males who could do her some serious damage. Powerful because they both had impressive erections. Because of her.

She held onto that thought, using it to boost her confidence. Like Beastly had said, they were all on the same page, so why delay things any further? The only problem was...

"Hmm, where to start?" She hadn't meant to say the words out loud, but they drew a laugh from both men.

"Well, you've got two hands, haven't you?" Beastly said, smiling at her. This time his eyes seemed to echo the sentiment. "Why don't you make good use of them?" He nodded towards his cock, then his brother's.

Belle took the hint. Taking Beastly's cock in her right hand, and The Beast's in her left, she marvelled at how her fingers didn't meet her thumbs around their girth—not even close. These were very big boys, and they were going to be inside her. She wasn't sure of the where or the how, but for now, it didn't matter. Each hand held a large, eager cock, and Belle bathed in the pleasure of knowing just how much each man wanted her.

As she stroked, she twisted her head to the right, then the left, taking in each of their expressions. Beastly was watching her hand on his cock, a grin on his face. The Beast had his eyes closed, clearly lost in bliss.

"Hey," she said, startling both men out of their lost-in-pleasure zones, "what about me? Don't I get any pleasure?"

Beastly was the first to react. He removed her hand from his cock and rolled on to his side, facing her. "You're absolutely right, dear girl. I was just so enjoying the sight and the sensation of your hand on my dick."

The Beast mirrored his brother's movements, and Belle turned at the sound of his voice near her ear. "Me too, but I'm kind of glad you stopped. Much more of that and I'd have come in your hand." He paused, and Belle swore she saw a wash of colour staining the skin high on his cheeks, above his beard. He shrugged. "It's been a while."

She smiled at him, then turned to Beastly, who seemed to be the instigator of their filthy tryst. "So, what next?"

"Well," he said, shifting down the bed and settling himself between her thighs, "as you so rightly pointed out, it's your turn for some pleasure."

With that, he spread Belle's legs and slipped his tongue between her swollen labia. She gasped, and barely had time to process what was happening when The Beast moved so he had access to her breasts. Latching onto one with his mouth, he took the other in his large hand and began to stimulate both.

Belle's pleasure was intense. More than intense. It was explosive. So much so that...

"Oh... oh... oh... I'm going to... come!"

Neither man reacted. They simply carried on with what they were doing until Belle's orgasm hit, making her writhe and thrash beneath them like a wildcat. Wave after wave of sublime feelings crashed through her body, and by the time she'd recovered sufficiently to become aware of her surroundings once more, the brothers had both donned condoms and were waiting for their next move.

"You're eager," she said, addressing both of them with a lazy smile.

"Of course we bloody are," Beastly said, pulling her up onto his lap, "that's the hottest thing we've ever seen."

With that, Beastly manoeuvred Belle, positioned his cock at her entrance, and without pomp or ceremony, pulled her down onto him. She threw her arms around his neck, letting out a guttural moan as he stretched and filled her pussy. Taking a couple of seconds to acclimatise to his size, Belle began to rock on his shaft, but Beastly stopped her.

"Wait," he said. "There's someone else who wants you too, remember."

Twisting to look over her shoulder, she watched as The Beast lubed up his thick cock, then squirted another generous blob of fluid onto his fingertips, which he then pressed into her crack. Quickly, efficiently, he made her rear hole ready for him, then crawled up close behind her and murmured into her ear. "You okay with this?"

Belle nodded, trying to reassure herself as much as him. She was no stranger to anal, but she'd never had both her holes filled at once, especially not by such large shafts. But then, she told herself, today was a day of firsts. And so far, it had been fucking incredible. She forced herself to relax against the additional invasion, and buried her face in Beastly's neck until the initial pain of the penetration passed. It did so quickly, and soon Belle was being fucked so hard and fast that she could barely see straight. She squeezed her eyes shut and held on for the ride.

She lost count of the amount of times she came. Her muscles ached from their repeated clenching, and her throat was hoarse from the groans and screams. Soon, a grunt in her ear and the cessation of movement from behind her indicated that The Beast was coming. Beastly had clearly been holding on until last as he followed immediately afterwards, and Belle went limp as she enjoyed the feeling of engorged, spurting cocks emptying themselves inside her.

It was just as the three of them were spiralling into blissful oblivion that she noticed Beastly's face. Normally so perfect, so attractive, it had now adopted a new expression. No, it was more than an expression. It had... transformed. Into something she couldn't quite comprehend. Something... Beastly.

A movement close by stirred Belle from her slumber. She opened her eyes and grinned as she looked upon the beautiful face of Beastly. Gone was the transformation she'd seen, and she decided it had all been in her lust-fuddled mind. The memories of the most incredible fuck of her life came rushing back, and she turned to gaze upon her other lover, The Beast. Only, he was The Beast no more. Sitting up sharply, and looking from one brother to the other, Belle could barely believe her eyes. Why... they could be twins!

The man that she thought was Beastly opened his eyes and grinned at her. "Hello, beautiful. Everything all right?"

He seemed different, somehow. Warmer, more genuine, but she didn't have time to process why.

"What do you think?" she said, jerking a thumb in the direction of the other sleeping man, who was the spitting image of the one she was looking at.

Beastly craned his neck to look around her. His smile widened, and he flopped back onto the pillow. "Ah, that. I guess we have a lot of explaining to do, huh?"

"Too right you fucking do," she snapped. She scrambled out of bed and began pulling her clothes back on. She couldn't hold a proper conversation with these men while they were all stark naked.

Beastly woke his brother and they both pulled on jeans. The three of them made their way downstairs, where Belle stood in the hall, tapping her foot impatiently.

Urging her to hear them out, Beastly launched into his tale. Had she not seen the evidence with her own eyes, Belle never would have believed it. Turns out the men were, in fact, twins, but they'd been cursed. Years ago, an old woman had come to their door trying to sell them something, and they'd turned her away. She'd started chanting strange words at them until they slammed the door in her face.

The following morning, The Beast—who was in fact called David—had been so covered in hair that he hadn't recognised himself. And every time he tried to cut it, it just grew back. Over time, it had made him incredibly grumpy and prone to fits of temper.

Beastly—otherwise known as Tom—hadn't immediately noticed any difference in himself. That was until he laid eyes on his brother, and instead of freaking out, had merely given a thin smile, and commented, "Guess that bitch got us good, huh?"

It was then he'd known that something wasn't right. He'd become a cold, uncaring bastard. It wasn't until they'd tracked the witch down that they'd discovered what exactly the curse entailed, and how to undo it.

"And that's when we knew we were royally screwed," David said. "Because she said we had to find a girl who would love us both. Only she meant love in terms of have sex with, and both as in both together. At the same time. I gave up hope immediately. I knew Tom would have no trouble getting a lady—he still had his looks, after all, and women don't seem to mind shagging utter bastards—but me? Nobody would see past the crazy hair and beard and see me as a worthy bed partner. Until you, that is. Thank fuck for you, Belle!"

"Glad to be of service," she said, as she retrieved the bag of catalogues from the hall floor. Moving towards the front door, she opened it, both ready and reluctant at the same time to leave the two men behind. She believed their story to be true, and part of her wanted to drag them back to bed for round two, but she really needed some time to get her head around things.

"Come back and see us again?"

She wasn't sure which one of them had spoken, but she turned and smiled at the sight of them standing there, wearing nothing but jeans and looking well and truly fucked. Which they were, she surmised. And that was down to her. Though of course they'd had a hand in it too. Four hands in fact, which had been all over—and inside—her body. Groping, pinching, caressing, teasing...

She shook her head before she disappeared into dirty fantasy land. Grinning at them both and moving out of the door, she said, "Oh, you can bet on it."

Magic and curses be damned. Those boys were damn good lays and she wasn't going to give them up in a hurry.

Her Majesty's Back Garden

From the moment Gavin whispered the saucy suggestion into my ear, I couldn't get it out of my mind. It was both highly inappropriate and incredibly risky, but that's what made it so deliciously appealing.

I tried not to let my excitement show – the last thing I needed was for my body language to appear skittish or suspicious. The number of CCTV cameras and security guards around the palace meant I'd be thrown into the Tower of London in the blink of an eye if they thought I was dodgy. Okay, well maybe not the *Tower,* but whatever it was that HRH Queen Elizabeth II's highly trained security personnel did to people they believed to be a threat to the monarch's safety, and that of her property.

I was no threat to anyone, never mind the Queen. I happen to really like the Royal Family – I wouldn't have paid to come on a visit to Her Majesty's official residence otherwise, would I?

Based on Gavin's devious plan, the worst I might do is tread on a couple of plants, or break a twig, or something.

For the remainder of our visit around Buckingham Palace, Gavin and I acted normally, albeit with the occasional grope and salacious wink when no one was looking.

By the time we arrived at the exit of the grand house, I was seriously horny. I took Gavin's hand, dragged him past the tearoom and out into the gardens. We had to find somewhere private—well, as private as you could get with thousands of visitors a day passing through—and quick.

It had been Gavin's idea, so naturally he was as enthusiastic as me, but I don't think he'd expected me to go for it in the first place. I slowed down after a couple of funny looks from people alerted me to the fact that we were drawing attention to ourselves. They probably thought we'd nicked a vase, or a painting. I had a vision of Her Maj shouting "Ooorrrf with their heads!" and giggled.

"What?" Gavin said, taking control and pulling me towards a bench – one of the many lining the path through the grounds. We sat down.

I told him what I'd been laughing at, and he laughed too, before cutting off my mirth by leaning in for a long, sensual kiss. It was deep, and delicious, and it sent tingles through my body from head to toe. We broke apart only when we heard someone coming towards us, and I gasped for breath as my heart raced. My imagination and the anticipation had ensured that my pussy was damp, but the kiss, and then the positively predatory look on Gavin's face meant I was seriously slick. I suspected that before long my juices would soak right through my underwear and I'd end up with a wet patch on the crotch of my jeans. Classy.

"Come on," Gavin said, looking around, "everyone's gone." He stood, then reached down and tugged me up by my elbow.

"W-where are we going?" I asked, my nerves threatening to show as he moved quickly behind the bench we'd been sitting on and into the trees and bushes, pulling me along with him.

"Somewhere nobody can see us, of course," he replied, releasing my arm and leading us deeper into the gloom cast by the trees, "but remember, if anyone walks past, they'll still be able to hear us, so you'll have to be quiet."

I nodded, which was stupid, as Gavin was in front and couldn't see my face. Then he stopped suddenly, causing me to bump into him. I exclaimed, and he turned and gave me an apologetic smile before saying quietly, "This is the place."

I looked around. There was plenty of cover on three sides of us, and on the fourth was a very high wall – which I presumed was the perimeter wall for the estate. The hustle and bustle of London lay just beyond. I continued to examine the area, convinced there were security cameras hanging from every other branch, and snipers on all the others. If there were, I couldn't see them, so I turned to Gavin and grinned, my horniness overriding any misgivings.

"Okay," I said, "let's do this!"

He responded by walking towards me, grabbing my hips and backing me up to a tree. I was trapped between rough bark and my husband's hard body. It was lush. Then he kissed me again, and if I'd thought the snog on the bench was hot; that was nothing. Gavin seemed to pour every ounce of passion and need he had into that kiss, and I could do nothing but enjoy it. And that was just fine.

I reached around and grabbed Gavin's muscular arse cheeks, and pulled him even more tightly to me. His eager erection pressed insistently into my stomach, and I had to concentrate hard on not moaning with pleasure.

Gavin's tongue pushed against my lips, and I opened my mouth eagerly to admit it. It slipped sensually against my own, twisting, tickling and mock-fighting until I was almost weak with lust. He shifted his hands from my hips and cupped my face, and then proceeded to suck and nibble at my bottom lip until my pussy throbbed and my clit ached, desperate for attention.

But it seemed that despite our precarious position, Gavin was in no rush to get full on down and dirty. When I thought about exactly what our position was, thrills of excitement ran through my body. It was crazy, yet incredibly arousing. What would happen if we got caught? I had some vague information in my head about indecent exposure which could lead to arrest. But this was a special circumstance—we were in the Queen's back garden, for fuck's sake! Would that make the crime even graver? Would we be dragged before the monarch herself to be given a punishment befitting the offense?

The weird thing was, at that moment in time, I didn't really care. The sex hormones rushing through my veins were obviously short circuiting the part of my brain that dealt with common sense and decency. And giving a shit. All I cared about was getting off – and soon.

By the time Gavin released my bottom lip, it felt hugely swollen and sensitive, and I seriously wanted him to give the same treatment to my clit. But it seemed it was not to be—not yet, anyway—instead his mouth pressed gentle kisses and nibbled the skin of my throat as he worked his way down to my collarbone, and from there, to my cleavage.

Pushing my breasts together, he gazed upon the deep valley that he'd created between them, then looked up at me with a devilish grin. "Nice tits, love."

I giggled, tangling my fingers in his dark hair. "Glad you think so, but this isn't the time or place to get them out. Maybe later, eh?"

"Bugger later," he replied, grabbing the hem of my top and pulling it up, then flipping down the cups of my bra, "I want to get my hands and mouth on these babies right now."

My words of protest were stopped in their tracks as he palmed one tit and sucked the tip of the other into his hot, wet mouth. I've always had the most sensitive boobs, and Gavin knew it—relentlessly tasting and caressing my plump flesh until I had to grit my teeth with the effort of staying silent. He swapped nipples, teasing one with his mouth while his hand pinched and twisted the other. My jaw started to hurt, but I daren't make a noise. I could hear people chattering and laughing as they walked along the path just a few metres away, and it wouldn't take much to send a do-gooder scurrying off to grass us up to one of the guards that patrolled the grounds.

Suddenly, Gavin moved his free hand between my legs and ground it against my crotch. It was so quick and unexpected that my reaction slipped out before my brain had time to catch up. "Ohhhh!"

We both froze, and Gavin snapped his head up to look at me, his eyes wide. "What happened to staying quiet, Jill?" he whispered.

"Sorry," I murmured back. "You just took me by surprise, that's all. I don't think anyone heard us, anyway."

We waited a good few seconds in silence, listening for the sound of approaching footsteps or indignant voices. There was nothing. We waited a little longer, just to be sure. Then, sure that my cock up hadn't attracted any unwanted attention, Gavin grinned at me and turned his attention back to my breasts.

Our brief intermission had done little to dampen my arousal, and I was quickly gripping onto Gavin's hair for dear life as he continued to pleasure me. I squeezed my eyes closed, leaned my head back against the tree and enjoyed.

This time I was more prepared for the touch between my legs, and I welcomed it by shuffling my feet apart, giving him better access. Before long I was at fever pitch; so horny and so desperate for orgasm that the need made me grumpy.

"Gavin," I ground out, without opening my eyes, "please will you make me come? You're driving me fucking crazy here."

He pulled my flesh out of his mouth with a pop, and chuckled quietly. "Getting to you, babe, is it? Well, I'll have to do something about that, won't I? Can't have my wife going without, can I?"

"No," I replied instantly, "you can't."

With that, Gavin straightened up and pressed a kiss to my lips. I opened my eyes and grinned as he undid the button and zip of my jeans and pushed his hand into the opening, slipped beneath my underwear—which was sodden—and *finally* touched my pussy. I let my hands drop from his head and gripped his biceps, tightening my hold as he began to finger me. Almost instantly, he arched his wrist—damn awkward in the limited space he had in my jeans—and sought my G-spot. I sucked my bottom lip into my mouth, literally biting back the "Fffffffuck!" I wanted to let out.

Teasing bastard that he is, he heightened my pleasure and equally my agony as he manoeuvred his thumb so it pressed against my clit. I moved my head forward, settling my mouth into the crook between his neck and shoulder and pulling the material of his t-shirt between my teeth. If I couldn't shout and scream my pleasure, I'd sure as hell bite it out of his top.

It was then, just as Gavin really went to work on my clit and G-spot simultaneously, making me fling my arms around his back and grip so hard I'm surprised he could breathe, that I had my first climax in the grounds of Buckingham Palace. I bit harder into Gavin's t-shirt as the blissful yet incredibly powerful tingles of pleasure spread throughout my body. My cunt twitched and gripped my husband's thick fingers, and I felt more juices run out of me to join the others already coating his hand and my knickers. I sucked in breaths through my nostrils and slumped against him as I rode out my orgasm.

I'd barely had time to recover when he gently pushed me back to lean against the tree again, and reached down to undo his own jeans. He let them drop around his ankles, and his boxer shorts quickly joined them. His cock bobbed slightly, ready and raring to go, with a bead of pre-cum seeping out. Before I had chance to reach out and stroke his shaft, maybe bend to lick the salty liquid from its tip, he grabbed my hips and turned me around to face the tree.

"Drop your jeans and knickers and bend over, baby."

I didn't need to be told twice. As soon as I was in position, Gavin shuffled right up behind me, aimed his cock at my cunt and sunk it in. He was soon balls-deep inside me and holding onto my fleshy hips for leverage, as I braced myself against the tree.

This time, there was nothing available to stifle my moans, and I didn't dare use one of my hands because if Gavin started fucking me hard, I'd probably end up head butting the trunk. And that would never do. I just gritted my teeth again and hoped that I'd be able to keep quiet.

After a couple of seconds where we both adjusted to the sensations below our waists, Gavin began to rock his hips, fucking me slowly at first, then faster. I knew he wouldn't go too fast because then the force of our bodies slapping together would make too much noise. He continued at a brisk pace, and my eyes rolled back in my head as his shaft rubbed against my G-spot, sending shivers running down my spine.

Despite the fact our fuck wasn't as fast and furious as normal, I knew that the risky situation had to be getting to Gavin, too, and that he wouldn't last too much longer. The sight of my white arse wobbling with every movement was probably driving him crazy, too.

My suspicions were confirmed when he reached a hand around to play with my clit. He leaned himself across my back so his lips were close to my ear, and whispered, "I'm going to come any minute now, babe."

I said nothing, just nodded my head frantically as he picked up his pace on the swollen bud at the apex of my vulva. He pressed and rubbed and pinched it, and I felt the resultant pressure building in my abdomen, behind a dam that would burst and send me spiralling into bliss once more.

Gavin continued to fuck me with small, jerky movements, forcing him deep inside my pussy, his glans butting against my cervix. I teetered on the very edge of another climax, but my husband beat me to it. He gave one final thrust and stilled, the hand that still gripped my hip tightening, his fingers digging into my skin in a delicious mix of pleasure and pain. Then I felt his cock twitch and leap, and the warm cum he released inside me.

His ministrations on my clit had paused briefly as he came, but now he redoubled his efforts, ensuring that my orgasm wasn't far behind. And it wasn't. The dam finally burst, and I bit my lip, screaming the expletives I would normally use loudly inside my head. I slumped against the tree, inadvertently allowing Gavin's cock to slip out of my pussy. I knew there was no time to waste, so I shook my head to try and get rid of my post-orgasm haze and bent down, feeling shaky, to pull up my underwear and jeans. Once I was done up, I put my bra and top back the way they were supposed to be, smoothed my hair, and turned to face Gavin.

We beamed at one another, united in giddy happiness at the success of our illicit fuck. He'd pulled himself together, too, and we moved in for a quick kiss before holding hands and creeping back towards the path. Peering carefully between the trees and bushes, we waited until the coast was clear before darting out and leaving the premises as quickly as possible, laughing all the way to the Tube station, and beyond. We could hardly believe we'd gotten away with it, and watched the news for several days afterwards, half-expecting there to be some CCTV footage of two people getting up to no good in Her Majesty's back garden, and asking for people to come forward and identify us. Thankfully, nothing of the sort happened.

Several months later, my mind often wanders to that day, and that crazy encounter. It's no wonder, really, because it was so deliciously naughty, and probably the hottest sex of my life. That, and the fact I've got a constant reminder.

I look down at my swollen stomach, stroke a hand across it and smile.

We've just had the results back. It's a girl.

We're going to call her Elizabeth.

Whatever would Her Majesty think?

It Takes All Sorts

In the past month, my life has been changed completely. Mostly my sex life, but the rest of my existence has been mind-blowingly altered, too. And all because of a bloody book.

I'd been out with the lads one Friday night after work, seeing off a colleague that was leaving. Things had gotten a little boring, and I was feeling horny, so I cried off and headed home, without telling Sue I was on my way. Me being home earlier than expected would be a lovely surprise. I hardly ever came home early.

It was a surprise, all right. I crept in, managed to get all the way up the stairs and to our bedroom door without being heard. I flung it open, grinning widely, proud of myself for not arriving home in an inebriated state. Sue barely glanced up from her position in the bed, propped up against the pillows. She clung to her eReader for dear life, her gaze flicking left to right, down, left to right, at what seemed like an impossibly fast speed. How could she even be taking in the words?

"Hi, babe. I came home early. I missed you." I was trying to get on her good side, hoping for some horizontal action, and I was under no illusions that Sue knew that, too.

"Let me just finish my chapter. I'm really into this." This time, she definitely didn't glance up from the digital page. Fucking hell, what was so engrossing that she couldn't even be pleased I'd come home early, and not stinking of booze? Well, not stinking too badly, anyway.

Shrugging, I emptied my pockets onto the dresser, then headed into the en-suite. Pulling off my clothes, I dropped them into the wash basket and then hopped into the shower. By the time I emerged, she was bound to have finished her bloody chapter, wasn't she? And I'd arrive back in the bedroom all clean and smelling nice... I was in with a chance, wasn't I?

Just then, the door to the shower opened and a naked Sue clambered in. You could have picked my jaw up off the floor. It had been a while since we'd done anything beyond missionary between the sheets, so the fact she had joined me under the spray was both shocking and a cause for celebration.

"Hello gorgeous," I said, determined not to let my surprise show. "I'm very glad to see you here. And so is someone else." I indicated my cock, which was already stiffening. "What's the occasion?"

She shrugged, reaching over to grab the shower gel, squeezing out a large dollop and spreading it across my chest with one hand as she used the other to put the container back. "I just felt like it, that's all. It's been a while since we've had some... fun." Grinning wickedly, she let her hands trail lower on my torso, until they were mere millimetres from my pubic hair.

"Um... okay." I still wasn't sure where her sudden enthusiasm for "fun" had come from, but I certainly wasn't complaining. Or questioning it. "Well I'm definitely up for some fun. What do you have in mind?"

Her suggestion was definitely not what I'd been expecting.

"Y—you want me to tie you up? Then use your vibrator on you?" I tried hard not to let my voice turn into something only dogs could hear, but I don't think I succeeded.

"Yep," she replied decisively. "Then maybe some other kinky stuff. Blindfolding, rough sex, spanking..." Sue appeared unaware of my reaction as she spouted off her list without batting an eyelid. I couldn't keep my questions in any longer.

"Sweetheart. That all sounds wonderful, and very, very arousing. In fact, I think my cock may explode with you just talking about it. But I can't help but wonder, what's brought this on? Have you been reading magazines again?"

"Not exactly." The wicked grin appeared again, sending a fresh burst of arousal coursing through my body. My cock was now so hard I suspected a breath whispering across its surface would be enough to make me come. "I've been reading this... book. An erotic book. It's kind of kinky. About BDSM and stuff."

Now my eyebrows made a break for my hairline. "An erotic book? That's where this has all come from? It must be a good read."

"Oh, it is. Very good. I'm only about halfway through and it's gotten me so damn horny. And given me lots of ideas. That's all right, isn't it darling? Me getting ideas, I mean."

"If they involve sex, then yes. Though we're not having sex with anyone else." I was determined to stand my ground on that one. So far, I liked my wife's ideas. I'm just a man, after all. But if her plans became too wild, I'd have to put a stop to it.

"No, no, definitely not. Just us, sweetheart. Well, us and perhaps some new toys..." Her hand was around my cock now, deliciously soapy and pumping up and down at a maddeningly slow pace. Just as well, really. Any faster and I'd be spunking. It was taking all of my will power to hold on as it was.

"Y—yes, okay. Anything you want, sweetheart. Buy whatever you like," I ground out, wishing she'd get on with it.

"Oh, thank you, Ellis. You're so kind. And generous. And sexy." Her grip tightened, and she stroked me faster.

"Uh, hey, babe. Good as that is, carry on and I'll come."

"That's the idea," she purred. "Come for me now, and we'll get washed up, then head to bed. You can use the ties from our dressing gowns for now. And one of your ties to blindfold me."

The visual of my wife spread-eagled on our bed, her wrists bound, and her eyes covered up so she couldn't see what I was going to do, was too much. One more stroke of her slippery fingers and I was done. I gave over to the pleasurable sensations, the cum boiling in my balls then shooting up and out of my shaft. I grunted and swore as my cock leapt and twitched in Sue's hand, painting her porcelain skin with my jism.

By the time I recovered, she'd already rinsed off and slipped out of the cubicle. I did the same, then quickly located her in the bedroom. She'd twisted her hair up on the top of her head—presumably so it was out of the way—and lain back on top of the duvet. Now she curved her lips up coquettishly, and beckoned me over.

"Hang on, gorgeous. I need to get the props."

"Of course, Sir. Sorry, Sir."

Her words stopped me in my tracks, and despite the fact I'd only just had an orgasm, my cock started to awaken again. Christ, what was going on here? Was she expecting me to dominate her as well as tie her up and blindfold her? Were they the same thing? Or not? I had no fucking idea, so I guessed I'd have to work it out as I went along.

"I should think so, too," I replied as sternly as I could. "Now just wait there like a good little girl, otherwise you'll get my belt."

Fucking hell, talk about nought to pervert in one second! Apparently I had it in me. Now I just had to let it out. Hurriedly, I grabbed a tie from the hanger inside the wardrobe, then moved to the bedroom door and relieved our robes of their binds, too. I didn't have enough materials to secure Sue's ankles, as well as her wrists, but it didn't matter. Not this time. She wanted it and she wanted it fast, so that's what she was going to get.

Walking back over to the bed, I wordlessly moved over to one side, looped one of the dressing gown belts around the post at the corner of the bed, secured it, then reached for Sue's wrist. She gave it willingly, and I tied it up, making sure it wasn't too tight, but also that she couldn't get free. I was sure it was part of the rules of tying people up, but to me, it was just common sense. I repeated the process on Sue's other side.

Then I dropped the towel that was around my waist and clambered onto the bed, my stiff cock bouncing in front of me, slapping against my stomach. I watched my wife's gaze follow its movement, wondering if I was going to straddle her head and fuck her mouth, push her ample breasts together and engage in a tit wank, or settle between her legs and sink into her cunt.

Whatever I was going to do, she wouldn't know until I did it. Leaning down, I captured her lips with mine, pressing hard against her, plundering her mouth with my tongue, rough, fast, possessive. I carried on for a while, pulling away only when I thought she'd be breathless and, hopefully, dizzy with lust. Then, without giving her chance to respond, I held the tie out.

"Lift your head."

To her credit, she obeyed, and I quickly put the makeshift blindfold in place, once again checking it wasn't too tight, and also that she couldn't see over or under it. Once satisfied, I clambered back off the bed, deep in thought. All these new kinky ideas had come from some book, and I wanted to make them a reality. But I wasn't entirely sure what to do next. Something more inventive than just fucking her—even though the fact she was bound already added a whole new dimension to our bedroom activities.

Part of me wanted to grab her eReader and have a look, but she'd hear me, work out what I was doing. And I wanted to be more inventive than that anyway. To surprise her. Impress her. Turn her on. Make her come.

Glancing around the bedroom, I searched for another prop. Something to make her erotic fantasy come to life. What else had she mentioned? Rough sex. Spanking...

My gaze alighted on the large, flat-backed hairbrush on the dresser, and I grinned. I hurried over and retrieved it, then returned to where my wife waited, trussed up and ready for hot sex. For kink. Well, she'd asked for it.

Hoping like hell I didn't get it wrong and fuck everything up, I joined her on the bed once more, then flipped the brush so the bristles were facing downwards. Then I began sweeping it over her skin. Of course, she'd now know exactly what implement I wielded, but hopefully the sensation would outweigh the lack of surprise. Her moans and wriggles, her luscious parted lips certainly confirmed my suspicion, anyway.

Continuing to tease and tantalise her with the hairbrush, I used my other hand to dip between her legs. Even before I'd touched her, I could feel the heat emanating from her core, and my cock hardened further in response. Delving between her swollen lips, I quickly discovered just how wet she was, and had to resist the temptation to discard my weapon and bury myself inside her. God, she was hot, tight and very wet. And I was determined to make her even more so before I was done.

She was as ready as she was ever going to be. After a couple more circuits with the bristles, I flipped the brush and abruptly landed a slap on her right thigh. Sue yelped, jerked, then moaned. The skin bloomed pink, the colour standing out against her pale skin. I gave her a matching blow on the other thigh. More noises, first voicing pain, then pleasure.

"Do you want more, little girl?" I wanted to be sure, without breaking out of my new bossy persona, that I wasn't hurting her too much. I figured she'd let me know if I was, but hey, it was my first time. I had to double check.

She nodded frantically, and I shrugged. "Okay. You asked for it."

I followed my words with a series of slaps all over her thighs, belly and breasts. Basically anywhere that was fleshy. The said flesh rippled with every blow, and I watched, fascinated by what I was doing, by what I was leaving behind. Sue's thighs had now gone from pink to red, and the rest of her delicious curves were catching up rapidly.

Before long, I decided to stop. My wife was gasping and panting, her cheeks—the ones on her face, that was—were red, her gasps and moans mutated into one long wail. I was pushing her close to the edge, I suspected, and I didn't want her to go over it. Not that edge, anyway. Climax I would deliver, but not an excess of pain.

Turning the brush on its end, I quickly insinuated it between her thighs and slipped it into her pussy. It met with no resistance whatsoever, given its slim size and the slickness of her. She growled, murmured, purred. Happy sounds. Pleasurable sounds.

I began fucking her with the handle of the brush. Slow and languid at first, then faster and harder, until I knew she was close to climax. Shoving her closer, and closer, I waited until she was a hair's breadth away, then I used my free hand to pinch her clit between finger and thumb. That was it. With a shriek, my wife descended into orgasmic bliss, her body bowing, her cunt grabbing at the brush, threatening to pull it inside. I removed it and quickly replaced it with my still-hard cock.

Immediately I was enveloped by the delicious undulations of her internal walls, sucking me in deeper, until my balls pressed against her nether lips. The waves were dying out as she rode out her orgasm, but I wasn't worried. I'd give her another before I came.

Remembering what she'd said about rough sex, I got myself into a position where I could thrust hard, fast and deep, and did just that. I'd always been conscious of hurting her by going too hard or deep, but she didn't protest, and I reminded myself I was giving her what she wanted. Giving my beautiful, sexy, horny wife what she'd asked for.

Letting go fully, I gave it everything I'd got, pounding her tight hole and hoping she'd get off before I lost myself to my own orgasm. If I hadn't already had one, I'd have been much more worried. But I could hold on, I could.

Shifting position ever so slightly, I made sure that my pubic bone rubbed against hers with every stroke, giving her swollen clit the attention it so desperately needed. Then I carried on until my hormones took over and all I could see was the end game. All I could feel was my cock, screwing a warm, slick hole. Squeezing my eyes closed, I tried my best to hang on, fearing I was about to disappoint Sue.

Then she saved me. Her cunt clenched tight, so tight around my shaft that I thought it would break off. Then she tumbled into another climax, seemingly a more intense one this time, as she grew silent and stiff, before letting out a wail that the neighbours three doors down probably heard. Her breasts bounced and wobbled as she thrashed, and it was only when I took a breath that I realised I, too, was coming. She'd yanked my release out of me so quickly, so forcefully, that somehow the pleasure was delayed.

It soon hit, hard and wonderfully, and I let out a few choice words of my own as ecstasy overtook me. My seed spilled into Sue's hot, hungry channel, and even mid-climax, I made the decision that it was the best sex I'd ever had. The best sex *we'd* ever had, I hoped. And, given these kinky books my wife had discovered, I knew that things would get even better.

Slipping out of her, I pushed the blindfold off her eyes, then untied her wrists. Flopping onto my back, I pulled her into my arms and pressed a kiss to her damp hair, wondering what other kinky delights were left in store for me in coming weeks and months.

It takes all sorts to get into BDSM, I suppose. It's not something that had ever crossed my mind, I must admit. But now I've done it, I thank God for that bloody book every damn day. In fact, I've started borrowing Sue's eReader at every opportunity, getting some ideas of my own. She'd never know what hit her.

Heat Upon Heat

Cecily couldn't tear herself away from the window. Not that she'd tried very hard. She should have been out there, under the sky, under the burning sun. Instead, she stood in the shadows of her bedroom, hoping like hell he didn't look up and see her standing there, watching him.

He was Ashley, the young man her aunt had hired to replace and paint her garden fence. He was only a few months older than Cecily, almost twenty-two, and he had a body to die for and was currently showing it off as he worked, topless.

She stared, utterly entranced, as he bent and lifted and stretched and painted. His muscles flexing and releasing, his body lithe, tight, strong. The sun beamed down on him, bathing him in light, highlighting the sheen of sweat that covered his beautiful body.

Cecily wanted to lick it off him. Lick every droplet of sweat like he was the world's tastiest ice-cream. Maybe then cover him in actual ice-cream and lick that off, too.

He looked like a Greek god, and she wanted to worship him. Pull those low-slung shorts down, then his underwear—if he wore any—and take his cock into her mouth, taste the perspiration and the sunshine. Suck and slurp at his shaft until he came in her mouth, filling her until she overflowed, dribbling his nectar down her chin and onto her chest.

It wasn't just his body that was delicious, though. His face was also perfection—brown hair that had that just-fucked look. Blue eyes that resembled the deepest ocean. Lips so sinful they should come with a warning. A jaw that appeared chiselled from the finest granite.

Cecily watched as Ashley made light work of the awkward fence panels. Her aunt was out, and therefore not supervising him, but he still worked as hard as he had been when Aunt Teresa was there. So that was good-looking, hard-working *and* honest. Was there no end to the man's perfection?

He paused, swiped the back of his hand across his forehead, removing the moisture that had gathered there.

Suddenly, Cecily imagined him naked in a cold shower. The chilly water sluicing all the stickiness away, cleaning him. So then she could make him all dirty again. Sweaty, panting. Rolling around in a tangle of crisp sheets, limbs linking, hair standing on end, rocking together.

He was so perfect, so godlike, that he had to be a spectacular fuck, too. His long thick cock would part her pussy lips, stretch her wide, ride her to a blissful climax. She'd hold on to his firm arse cheeks, wrap her legs around his, jerk her hips, pull him deeper, harder.

She couldn't help it; she pushed her hand down under the waistband of her shorts, into her knickers, touched herself. Her cunt was already wet and ready, swollen and slick with thoughts of the handsome man in the garden. Thoughts of him fucking her, thoughts of her fucking him.

She closed her eyes, let the sexy mental images take over, fill her mind, fill the blank canvas behind her eyelids. The fantasies became more graphic, more heated, and she moved her hand faster, stroked her distended clit harder, wishing she had something long and thick to stuff in her cunt as she masturbated to dirty imaginings of Ashley.

Her chest heaved, her breaths grew rapid as she teased her body closer and closer to orgasm, her imagination firing her up as much as her touch, if not more.

Ooh, she was nearly there; her body grew tight, a tingle began in her groin, radiated out. Just a few more strokes...

"Cecily?" A deep, sexy voice broke her reverie, her concentration. Her climax sunk like an anchor, into the depths of her disappointment. Stunned, she turned around, only snatching her hand from her knickers when it was too late. He'd already seen. Seen that she was wanking. At least he didn't know what about. Though her position at the window probably gave him a damn good idea. Fuck.

His gorgeous eyes darkened as he continued to look at her. A smile curved those sinful lips. "I just came to tell you I'm finished for the day." He stepped towards her. "But now I can see I'm not. Not by a long shot."

Cecily soon realised he was nothing like her fantasies. He was a million times better. He grabbed her and pushed her onto the bed, quickly covering her body with his. The heat from his sun-baked skin seeped through her thin vest-top and mingled with her own warmth. Heat upon heat, it threatened to melt her, to make her spontaneously combust.

And that was before he even kissed her. Once he captured her lips with his, slipped his tongue into her mouth and rocked his hips gently against hers, she was lost. The dampness in her knickers increased tenfold and she wanted nothing more than for her fantasies to come true. Right away.

She couldn't speak, couldn't voice her need as Ashley wouldn't stop kissing her. And when he eventually did, the things he did to her were so utterly decadent that he rendered her silent. His lips trailed down her chin, her neck, her chest. He tugged off her top, her bra and sucked and licked her until she was a writhing mass of need.

The shorts went, along with the sodden knickers. Ashley pressed his mouth to her cunt and within seconds he'd brought her back to the edge of the orgasm she'd lost when he walked in on her. She had no time to worry about her own sweat as his talented lips and tongue gave her what she so desperately wanted; a climax that far surpassed any she'd ever had by her own hand or by that of someone else.

Her Greek god had otherworldly skills, it seemed, and he spent the rest of the long, hot summer demonstrating them on her eager body. Demonstrations she happily returned.

The Unexpected Submissive

Evan pulled onto his drive and pressed the button on the remote control to open the garage door, drove in and parked the car. When the door finally swung shut, he heaved a sigh of relief. God, he was pleased to be home. He knew that many people would kill to be in his shoes and go to conferences and things abroad, but he'd just spent four days in Paris and had barely had a minute to himself. It was all work and no play. He'd certainly had no time for sightseeing, which sucked as Paris was one of his favourite cities. The conference schedule had been absolutely packed out and he'd attended every lecture he could—often having to choose between two running at the same time—as well as speaking at one session himself.

It had basically been: lecture, coffee, lecture, lunch, lecture, dinner, shower, bed. For four days. Except for the part where he'd been travelling, of course. And the flights hadn't been great, either. There'd been turbulence both ways and a delay going out. Evan was so exhausted when the conference drew to a close that he didn't bother with the last night he'd booked in the hotel. Instead, he'd packed his bags, checked out and got a taxi to the airport, intending to take the next flight home. Factoring in the time difference, he worked out he'd be home around 9pm. Just enough time for a soak in the bath and then to collapse into his nice comfortable bed. Then he had two days to recover before it was back to work on Monday. He could hardly wait. To recover, that was, not go back to work.

He entered the house through the internal garage door into the kitchen and locked it behind him. Grabbing a bottle of water from the fridge, he headed upstairs. He'd already eaten on the plane—though, as usual, it had been insubstantial and bland—so next on the agenda was the bath he'd been daydreaming about ever since he'd left the final lecture. He'd unpack his bag tomorrow.

Moving into his bedroom, he put the bottle of water down on the bedside table. Pulling his phone and wallet from his trouser pockets, he placed them down next to the water, then stripped off. Bundling his clothes into his arms, he made for the bathroom. Using his elbow to open the door, he entered the room sideways-on and dropped his clothes directly into the laundry basket. Then he turned to the bath.

His jaw almost hit the floor. For there, lying in the water-filled tub, was his cleaner, Rochelle. And, unless he was quite mistaken, she'd been masturbating. Her chest, neck and face were flushed, but he supposed that could be from the heat of the water. The hand trapped between her legs, however, was a dead giveaway. As was the expression on her face. Evan wasn't sure how it was possible, but she looked shocked, guilty and aroused all at once.

Several more moments passed where the two of them stared at one another in a stunned silence. Then Evan remembered that he was standing there, stark naked. And his cock had clearly taken note of the naked woman mere feet away, because it was starting to swell. He cupped his genitals quickly, then broke the silence.

"Rochelle, what are you doing masturbating in my bath?" The tone of his voice was much more chilled out than he felt.

"M—Mr. Hallett, I wasn't expecting you back until tomorrow!" Rochelle's dark chocolate eyes were wide, and her coconut-coloured skin looked even darker against the pale white of the bathtub. Her large breasts bobbed above the water, her nipples elongated and several shades darker than her skin.

"Clearly not. And that didn't really answer the question now, did it?" Force of habit wanted him to cross his arms, but he stopped himself just in time. He'd struggle to remain firm—for want of a better description—if Rochelle happened to notice his rapidly growing cock. The sight before him, and the thought of what she'd been up to, was terribly distracting. He'd always found his young cleaner attractive—in fact, it was part of the reason he'd given her the job. It certainly wasn't her credentials. She was inexperienced and had no references. But a friend of a friend had suggested her— the girl was at university and was struggling to pay her tuition and living costs, so she needed to work, too.

Despite the fact she was untried and untested, she'd proven to be a very good cleaner. Very efficient, and very thorough. She'd worked for him for several months now and he'd grown to trust her enough to give her a house key so she could clean while he was out. And now it seemed he'd made a mistake. For the girl was letting herself into his house all right—making herself at home and wanking in his bloody bath!

Rochelle still hadn't answered his question, and he suspected she wasn't going to. After all, what kind of explanation could one give for masturbating in one's boss' bath? Certainly not a satisfactory one.

"Okay, Rochelle. Fun's over. I came home early from my business trip, I'm exhausted and all I want to do is have a bath. And I arrive to find you using my home as though it were your own." He grabbed the dressing gown which hung on the back of the bathroom door and held it out to her. "Now get out."

She reached out and took the dressing gown, then scrambled from the bath and quickly wrapped it around her, tying the cord tightly. Instead of leaving, however, she gazed imploringly at Evan. "Please, Mr. Hallett, forgive me. I only used your bath because the ones at my halls of residence are in such hot demand. You can't relax—you have to be in and out in twenty minutes, otherwise there will be other girls banging on the door and shouting at you. This is the first time I've done it. It's not a regular occurrence, I promise."

"Sounds delightful," he replied dryly, rolling his eyes.

"I am so sorry, Mr. Hallett. It will never happen again. I was going to clean it after I was done—you would never even have known I was here. Please don't fire me."

"Fire you?" He hadn't even thought of that—he was more put out than angry, since there hadn't really been any harm done. He'd planned to make her suffer by being mean to her the next few times he bumped into her, but he'd had no intention of sacking her. It's not like he'd caught her stealing, or anything. But now she'd put the idea into his head, he decided to play on her fear, just for a bit of fun. "I should, you know." He suppressed a smile as her eyes widened and she wrung her hands together despairingly. "But I'm not going to. Instead, I'm going to punish you."

When the last sentence came out of his mouth, he realised how pervy it sounded. But of course it was too late to take it back. When he observed Rochelle's reaction, however, he was suddenly very glad he'd said it. Her pupils grew larger and the rate of her breathing increased. Her chest heaved, and he was sure that beneath the terrycloth, her nipples were erect, too.

So, he had himself a sexually submissive employee, did he? That was very interesting indeed. Ideas whirled through his brain. He wondered if she was interested in him personally, just his dominant personality, or the idea of being punished. He figured it didn't really make a difference—if she agreed to his proposal then she was effectively giving her consent, and that was all that mattered. He was kinky, not a rapist.

His cock was now pressing insistently against his hand and

holding it down was really starting to hurt. He decided to let go of it—if Rochelle screamed and ran away, or slapped him, then he'd take that as a no and claim there'd been a misunderstanding. If she didn't, though, then he would make another move.

He removed his hand. Immediately, her gaze dropped to his crotch, and she raised her eyebrows. Then she looked back up at him, the corners of her mouth curving up just a little, and licked her lips. Well, he hadn't been expecting that. Not only was his cleaner a submissive—she was a saucy little bitch, too.

Taking her actions as a resounding yes, he asked her a question. "So you want me to punish you then, do you, Rochelle?" As far as he was concerned, that was her last chance to back out. He was a nice guy, not a pushover.

She nodded emphatically, and he gave what he hoped was a cool smile.

"Very good. Well, you can start by sucking my cock." Okay, so it wasn't exactly a punishment—well, maybe for some women, but probably not this one—but he was in charge, and he wanted her to suck him off. He needed to come, and then he could concentrate better and turn his mind to some more traditional, and wicked, chastisements.

Rochelle dropped immediately to her knees in front of him and grasped his shaft between her slim fingers. It twitched, and she flashed a grin up at him before stroking him slowly a few times, then pulling his foreskin back gently until he was completely exposed. Then she bent her head and flicked her tongue around the sensitive underside of his glans, concentrating on the frenulum. He gasped and fisted his fingers into her wet hair. He wasn't going to force himself into her mouth, but God, did he need something to hold on to. She'd barely touched him and already he felt himself rocketing towards climax. Well, it had been a while. Not to mention Rochelle was totally gorgeous, clearly good with her mouth, and the circumstances were very hot.

His groan filled the air and he rocked his hips gently, hinting that he wanted his cock to be inside her mouth. He wasn't going to push it any further, not just yet. He didn't know if she was submissive enough to simply take everything he gave, or whether she'd bite back—literally. Happily for Evan, Rochelle took it all in her stride, continuing to tease him for just a little longer before enveloping his shaft in the hot wetness. A strangled yelp escaped his lips as she sunk further onto him, until her nose was touching his pubic hair and he could feel her gag reflex squeezing around his glans. Wow, the girl really did know how to give good head.

It seemed she was enjoying it, too, as a glance downwards showed she had a hand between her spread thighs. The dressing gown prevented him from seeing exactly what she was doing, but his imagination more than filled in the gaps. Then a series of decidedly slick sounds confirmed his erotic imaginings to be true.

Unfortunately—or fortunately, dependent on which way you looked at it—Evan couldn't take any more. The totally unexpected erotic situation he'd found himself in, plus the fact he'd been so busy at the conference all week that masturbation had been off the menu, meant that he was more than ready to come. So he did. He couldn't help it; he tightened his grip on her damp locks and thrust deep into her throat a couple of times before letting out a howl that probably roused all the neighbourhood's dogs, and emptying his balls inside her mouth. If he was in a relationship where he had some deep feelings for the woman, or he knew she wasn't so keen on having spunk in her mouth, he'd have felt guilty about the amount he was unloading into her. But he didn't have deep feelings, he had dominant feelings and so he held Rochelle's head in place until he was done coming.

He needn't have bothered, though. It seemed Rochelle was a very good little submissive, and when she'd swallowed every drop of his ejaculate, she used her talented tongue to clean his softening shaft. As with her more traditional cleaning, she was very thorough and when she finally pulled away and looked up at him, seemingly awaiting her next orders, Evan suspected it wouldn't take much to get his cock hard again.

"Well done." He said, patting her on the head as though she were a small child or a family pet. "That was very good. But you're not off the hook yet."

Of course she wasn't off the hook—he had a beautiful and very willing woman kneeling at his feet. Why on earth would he end the fun after a single blowjob?

"Right," he said, buying himself some time so he could think of what to do next, "empty the bath and clean it, like you said you were going to. When it's spotless, take off the dressing gown, hang it back up, then come into the bedroom on your hands and knees and wait for my next command."

Turning on his heel, he left the bathroom and walked into his bedroom. Inside his head, he applauded himself. He had successfully bought himself some thinking time, without appearing to Rochelle as though he didn't know what he was doing. If he was truthful to himself, he was completely out of practice with all the domination stuff. His last relationship had not had the D/s element—which was why it hadn't worked out—and prior to that, the last time he'd played with someone like that had been... God, had it really been two years? No wonder he'd come so damn much. And why he was so rusty.

Sitting in the chair in the corner of the room, Evan leaned his elbows on his knees, steepled his fingers and propped his chin on them. What would he do next, when Rochelle crawled across his bedroom floor on her hands and knees, her delicious tits swinging below her, those lips at his mercy once more?

His thoughts whirled. There were just so many possibilities—each and every one of them helping to get his dick hard again—that he couldn't decide. The sounds of spraying and squeaking coming from the bathroom told him that he had a little longer to make his mind up—Rochelle was still hard at work scrubbing the bathtub.

After a few more minutes, his decision was made. He was going to get himself back into things by starting off simple, which also made sense because he didn't know how experienced Rochelle was, either. And who knew—if he played his cards right, she may even decide she wanted to play with him on a more regular basis. If that was the case, they could progress onto the harder stuff when they were both ready.

A little while later, he watched as Rochelle's head appeared around the door frame. She took note of where he was, then moved forwards on her hands and knees as he'd requested, heading towards him. Blood rushed to Evan's cock as he observed her naked form— her beautiful big curvy arse wiggling with every movement, the nipples of her pendulous tits elongated, pointing to the carpet she crawled across. He suddenly wanted nothing more than to bury his shaft between them—her tits or her arse, actually—trapping himself between the smooth, plump coconut-coloured flesh and pumping until his spunk decorated her skin.

But there was plenty of time for that. He had other plans for her bum first. Leaning back in the chair, he waited until she was kneeling in front of him once more and flashed her a cool smile. "My bath is clean?"

She nodded vigorously.

"Yes... Sir."

Shit. His dick leapt. He'd forgotten how much it turned him on when a woman called him Sir. Taking a deep breath, he forced himself to be calm. He didn't want to get too aroused. Not yet, anyway. There was something he wanted to do before he came again.

"Very good. I'll be checking it later to make sure you're telling the truth. If not, you'll be punished again. Understand?"

"Yes Sir." She lowered her head and her gaze.

"Excellent. Now, get up here and put yourself over my knees. Perhaps if it hurts to sit down for a week, you won't be tempted to use my facilities as though they were yours again. Come on."

The way Rochelle moved into the position he'd commanded indicated that she was no stranger to being put over someone's knees and spanked. He wondered just how experienced she was. But that was a conversation for another time. Right now he was going to make her arse—and his hand—red hot. He stroked her rear, grinning as he realised her skin was still a little damp from the bath. That would make his blows all the more painful for her.

He continued to sweep his hand lightly over her cheeks, relaxing her as much as possible. Then when the first blow came, she'd be more surprised. Probably. Before long his dick was so hard that he thought it would explode, and he decided to stop delaying, and start spanking.

What that, he lifted his hand and landed the first blow on Rochelle's curvy arse. She let out a hiss—more of shock than anything, the pain wouldn't have bloomed just yet—and jerked her hips forward, causing her to wobble on his legs.

"Hey," he said sharply. "Keep still. I haven't decided how many spanks you're going to get yet, but I can always keep increasing the number until you do as you're damn told."

He heard Rochelle suck in a trembling breath, then, "Yes, Sir. Sorry Sir."

"I should think so, too." He gave her a moment to wriggle back into position, then he really let loose on her. He barely paused between blows, raining spanks down on her arse until a wash of pink showed, then eventually grew closer to red. Given her natural skin tone, he figured that pinkish-red was quite an achievement. He'd teach the disobedient bitch to use his damn bath!

The more he beat Rochelle, the more confident he became that she was, in fact, an old pro at this kind of treatment. She didn't scream, didn't wail, and now, the only movements she made were the inevitable jerks caused by the force of his blows. He did, however, hear her sharp intakes of breath with every blow. She was good, but not infallible. Which was fine, actually, because he wanted to spank a flesh and blood woman, not a machine.

And spank her he did. He lost count of the times he brought his hand down on her quivering flesh, even having to swap hands occasionally as his right one grew numb, so heaven knew what her bottom felt like. Evan stopped only when he couldn't land another smack. His arms were tired, his hands sore and his cock was desperate to sink into some delicious warm girl flesh.

"Get up," he said suddenly, giving her a shove. She fell to the floor in a jumble of limbs, but to her credit she instantly recovered and moved to a kneeling position in front of him. He raised his eyebrows.

"Wow, you *are* a good girl, aren't you? Done this before then, have you?"

Rochelle nodded. "Yes, Sir."

"Well, you can tell me all about it some other time. Right now I absolutely have to fuck you, or I fear my balls will turn blue and drop off. Are you safe?"

"Yes, Sir. Free of STIs and on birth control."

"I'm very glad to hear it. Now get onto the bed on your hands and knees. Close enough to the edge that I can stand behind you and fuck your brains out."

She lowered her head in supplication, then got up and scampered across the room to do his bidding. Evan followed her quickly, standing behind her and admiring his handiwork. Her arse looked severely punished and she'd definitely be feeling the effects for a few days. His gaze was quickly drawn to the splayed pussy lips which were on full display, and was gratified to note that his new submissive was well and truly that, a submissive. And a masochist, at that. Her cunt glinted with juices. Without warning, he pushed a finger deep inside her and covered it with said juices, then pulled it out and sucked it into his mouth.

"Mmm. You taste good. You're very wet, my dear. Did you

enjoy your spanking?"

"Yes, Sir, I did. Very much." The tone of her voice told him that she wasn't just going through the motions, telling him what he wanted to hear; she meant every word.

"You horny little bitch. Let's see if you're still enjoying it when my body is slapping hard against your beautifully punished arse as I fuck you." He didn't give her chance to reply, instead moving right up behind her, gripping one hip and then grasping his shaft in the other hand. Butting the head of his cock up against her entrance, he spoke again.

"One day, my dear, I'm going to stick my dick up that tight little arse of yours, and you're going to like it. But for now, your juicy pussy will do." Evan marvelled at how quickly he'd gotten back on the horse, so to speak. It seemed his dominant persona and ability to talk dirty and issue threats had never gone away, they'd just been in hibernation. And thank fuck for that, because right now they were being called to the fore in a big way.

She was so wet that he met little resistance from her tight internal muscles as he pushed inside; they simply gave way, as submissive as the woman they were part of. Soon, he was buried in her to the hilt, his balls pressing against her body, already tingling with the need to come. He sucked in a deep breath, attempting to dampen down his desperation to climax.

It didn't work. After a beat, he figured that since he was the one in charge, it didn't matter when he came, whether it was after two seconds or two hours. If he came quickly then wanted to fuck Rochelle again five minutes later, that was exactly what he would do. If he wanted to fuck until they were both raw, that was fine too. It didn't matter. She was his new plaything and would submit to anything he did or requested of her. And he couldn't be any happier about it.

Rocking his hips slowly at first, then faster, Evan enjoyed the change of pace. He knew that if he teased himself to the brink, then denied himself, then did it again and again, by the time he actually came it would be explosive. And he couldn't think of a better way of celebrating the discovery of his unexpected submissive.

He became so lost in sensation that he was barely aware of anything else. He closed his eyes, watching the white dots that danced amongst the darkness behind his lids until his balls tightened for one final time, and he let go. With a roar, he fell into blissful oblivion as hot spunk pumped out of him and into Rochelle's cunt.

When he was finished, he slumped on top of her briefly, before rolling off to one side. After regaining some use of his muscles, he scrambled up the bed and settled back into the pillows. He looked at Rochelle, who was watching him, clearly unsure what to do next. He beckoned her, and when she came he folded her into his arms and pressed a kiss to her dark, tangled hair.

"Well," he said softly, "that was not what I expected to happen when I got home from Paris. But in all honesty, I can't say I'm sorry about it."

"No, Sir." She was snuggling into him comfortably, as though they were long-time lovers. Clearly she needed some kind of reassurance, and he was happy to give it. He kissed her hair again, and stroked her face.

"Rochelle, can I ask you something?"

"Yes, Sir. Of course."

"How was that for you? I haven't done anything like that for a long time, and I really laid into your arse. Speak freely."

"I've had worse masters than you, Sir. Much worse." The way she said it made him believe that she didn't think this was a bad thing—she was just stating a fact.

"Well," he said, noticing his cock stirring once more. It seemed he was insatiable when it came to Rochelle. "I'm only just getting started. My imagination is fertile and my body more than willing, so I'm sure before long I'll be climbing the ranks of your worst masters. In fact, I won't stop until I'm at number one. So, what do you think of that, young lady? Speak freely."

"Sir," she said, twisting to look at him with a wicked smile and a glint of excitement in her eyes, "I can't think of anything I'd like more. I think I'll use your bath without permission more often."

"I look forward to it."

Does He Know Me At All?

I stifle a sigh as I open the door to an enormous bunch of flowers with a pair of legs sticking out of the bottom. It's not the delivery person's—I say person because I currently have no idea if they're male or female—fault, after all. Not their fault that my ex-boyfriend really doesn't know me at all.

Realising I haven't yet spoken, I say, "Yes, can I help you?"

"Oh, sorry," a voice says. "I have a delivery for Miss Brooks."

"That's me." I reach out and carefully take the bouquet, stepping back to place it in my hallway. "Thank you."

"You're welcome." I see now that the delivery person is in fact a woman around the same age as me, hair pulled into a ponytail and a genuine smile on her face. "You're a lucky woman," she adds, gesturing to the flowers. "He must really love you. That's the most expensive arrangement we have."

"You have no idea," I reply, faking a smile.

"Bye then." She turns and heads back to her van.

"Thanks, bye."

I close the door, twist the key in the lock, then lean my head against the cool wood and let out the sigh I'd previously stifled. I meant the part about her having no idea in a sarcastic way, really, but I hadn't wanted her to know that. She was just being kind.

Finally, I pull myself together, pick up the flowers and take them into the kitchen. They're nice enough, if you like that sort of thing. Which I don't. If they're in a garden or a pot, yes. But cut them, and soon they'll die, withering away on a windowsill or a table. Such a colossal waste of money, especially since I don't sit at home looking at my windowsill or table all day. I have better things to do.

I just don't get the point of flowers, never have. They're a gesture, sure. But if you're going to make a gesture, an apology, a declaration of love or whatever, then for god's sake make an effort to find out what the intended recipient likes!

He should know better, he really should. If, after three years, he thinks that flowers will melt my heart and open my legs, then he's more clueless than I ever imagined.

The bouquet has served a purpose, though. They've made me

even more positive I made the right decision in breaking up with him. I mean, he bought me flowers, despite my mentioning on several occasions that I don't like them and that I think they're a waste of money. I shouldn't be surprised, though. Once, he took me to a seafood restaurant, totally forgetting my fish allergy. Another time, a trip to the cinema had seemed like a good idea, until I realised he'd booked tickets to a film starring an actor I loathe and despise—and that can't even act.

I'd tried so many times to work out whether he was just an idiot, or whether he was so wrapped up in himself that he didn't take any notice of what I wanted, what I needed. What I *liked,* for fuck's sake! Eventually, I gave up because I just couldn't figure him out, and had grown bored of trying to.

Pulling the cellophane from around the bottom of the bouquet, I realise they are already in a vase. Excellent, I haven't even got to pretend I know what I'm doing when it comes to flower arranging. I top up their water supply—I may not like them, but waste drives me crazy, so I'm not going to let them die needlessly because of my neglect—then head into the living room and put them on the windowsill.

Then I leave the room, still quietly fuming about my stupid ex-boyfriend and his even stupider attempts at getting me back. If he can't pull out all the stops, actually figure out what the fuck I want, then why the hell should I even consider it?

Shaking my head, I go into my bedroom and flop onto my big, soft bed, figuring I'll let myself be grumpy for an hour or so, then get on with my life. As I sink into the pillows, I come to the conclusion that I don't need that moron, anyway. Tragically, in three years he didn't really enhance my life in any way shape or form. He just pissed me off, frustrated me and bumbled along, oblivious.

My gaze is drawn to my bedside cabinet, which contains my other boyfriend. The one made of rubber, that's long and thin with cute little bunny ears and a bunch of buttons that make him do precisely what I want. Grinning, I roll towards the cabinet, pull open the door and retrieve the black silky bag. Opening the drawstrings, I take out the vibrator, giving one of the buttons a brief press to make sure the batteries have still got enough power to get me off. They have. Awesome.

I shift back to the centre of the mattress, temporarily abandoning the toy as I remove my jeans and underwear, not bothering about my socks or any of the clothes on my top half. I know my rubber boyfriend won't mind—he likes me no matter what I'm wearing, or not wearing. He's ready to go at any time of the day and recovers from an orgasm even faster than I do.

The best part, though, is the fact that he knows me. He knows me well, knows me intimately, goes where I direct him and doesn't damn well stop until I tell him to. There's no whinging if he doesn't get inside me for a while, and especially no complaints if I overuse him. Bless him, my rabbit-eared friend knows me best of all, probably better than I know myself, and I love him dearly for it.

Spreading my legs, I press the button to make my rubber boyfriend's ears vibrate, then lower him to my crotch, pressing the flexible protrusions gently against my clit. I jerk, the sensation too intense at first, but the more my nerve endings grow used to the stimulation, the harder I push the toy against my swelling nub. Soon, my juices begin to flow, but I wait a little longer, ensuring my pussy is good and wet before slipping the length of the vibrator inside.

It stretches me, just a little, but it feels good. So fucking good. The lumps and bumps rub me in all the right places, and that's before I even touch the other button, the one that makes the shaft rotate. Allowing the vibrations to tease and torment my clit for a while longer, racking my body with pre-orgasmic pleasure, I relish the sensations, the perfect sensations for a few seconds more, then more still.

After a couple of minutes, I decide it's time to ramp up the bliss, and I push that other button, letting out a yowl as yet more of my nerve endings are sparked, eventually setting fire to kindling which I know will be a slow yet delicious burn, resulting in my consumption. My battery-operated boyfriend does what he does best; tickling my clit into submission while my G-spot is stroked relentlessly until my toes curl.

I arch my back, the movement temporarily unseating the bunny ears from their perfect position on my swollen bud. They find their way back quickly, barely losing me a moment's pleasure and I continue to bask in the feelings of joy that are humming through my veins, my nerve endings, my every cell.

The moment of no return is approaching, I can feel it. I can't decide whether to let it come, or to delay it. Have my cake, or wait and hope it's a bigger cake when it arrives? I quickly come to the conclusion it doesn't matter either way. If I come, I can always go again. I know damn well my rubber boyfriend will oblige my needs, without hesitation, and with total relish.

I decide to go for sooner, rather than later. I need this climax, need it to wash over me, cover me, suspend me in perfect ecstasy. To thrust me into total oblivion.

Pressing the vibrate button again, I gasp as the shuddering grows faster. I quickly grow accustomed to the change in tempo and I fist my free hand into the duvet as my hormones take over, sending tingles rushing across every inch of my skin. The pleasure radiates out, then pulls back in to my abdomen, to my cunt, holding there for several long seconds, the pressure like water behind a dam wall.

A pause, a moment of nothingness, then the wall cracks, splinters, allowing not water, but bliss, perfect fucking bliss to overtake me, to pull cries from my lips, to send my body into spasm. As my toy rotates and vibrates on, my pussy clenches around it relentlessly for seconds on end, each gripping action forcing another delicious shiver across my skin.

When it becomes too much, I hit both buttons on the vibrator, instantly halting its actions, then I pull it out of me and drop it to the bed. Fortunately, I know he doesn't mind, that he'll forgive me, that he'll be ready to go again as and when I decide I am. Is there no end to his perfection?

My muscles relax and I sink deeper into the mattress and pillows, feeling buzzed and weightless all at once. Now my climax has been and gone, my mind wanders back to the colourful blooms sitting on my windowsill, all alone and neglected.

I snort, groping around for the rabbit once more. Fucking idiot would have been better off buying me batteries.

Without Question

I do it without question. Every single thing she asks of me. I relinquish all power, all responsibility. It is wonderfully freeing. It is sublimely beautiful. Just like her.

"Kneel," she barked. I did it. I dropped to my knees before her perfect form. Part of me wanted to look up, to drink in the sight of her standing there, hands on her hips, her body encased in shiny black leather. I knew I wouldn't lift my gaze, though. I couldn't. I have the utmost respect for my Mistress and never want to do anything to displease her. Especially since my Mistress is also my wife.

Ever since I got back from Afghanistan and met her in a restaurant, she's been testing me. Then, it was teasing my cock under the table while she was wearing sharp stilettos, bringing me to the very edge of climax, right there in the restaurant. Now, she occasionally takes over the role of my ex-commanding officer and treats me like some kind of new recruit.

"Now drop and give me twenty. No, scratch that. Make it forty."

It was clichéd, totally unoriginal, but it got me harder than I'd ever been in my life. After so long taking orders without question, it was impossible to change that aspect of my personality, which is why I'm so grateful that Cassie came into my life—permanently—when she did. She took over the role of the Army, directing me here, there and everywhere, helping me to move forward, to adjust to civilian life. Together, we took baby steps, and when I felt able to cope, she scaled back her bossiness and reserved it strictly for the bedroom. Or, you know, anywhere else we had sex. Which was everywhere.

It worked perfectly. Day-to-day life was mine to control, to live. But as soon as we slipped into a scene, I was completely submissive—just the way I liked it.

I closed my eyes as the sight of the carpet coming closer, then moving farther away was in danger of making me feel queasy. I obviously wasn't working hard enough, because a spike-heeled boot settled into the small of my back and pressed down. I hesitated for a millisecond, gathering all the strength I had, and continued with the press-ups. It was more difficult, of course, but it was also much more rewarding. Not to mention arousing. The shards of pain generated by the boot's heel sliced through my body, making my blood pump faster, harder, twisting my pleasure dial up to eleven. Thankfully my boxer shorts and jeans were tight enough to keep my cock under control, otherwise it would have gotten in the way as I lowered myself to the carpet.

I concentrated on keeping track of how many push-ups I'd done. If I fucked up and miscounted, I would be punished. And as much as I loved the punishments, I loved my Mistress and her delectable body more, and the sooner I satisfied her whims, the sooner she'd let me loose to play with her, pleasure her. Make her come.

"Very good," she eventually said, placing her foot back on the carpet. "You're getting so good at these impromptu fitness tests, Holden. I'll have to think of something different. More challenging." She fixed me with a stern gaze.

"Yes, Mistress. Whatever you say."

"Of course you'll do whatever I fucking say!" Like lightning, her hand left her side and slapped my face. The heat and the humiliation zipped immediately to my groin.

"Please," I murmured. Then louder. "Please!"

"Please what?" she said, putting a finger beneath my chin and yanking my head up. Her eyes flashed. My cock throbbed.

"Please can I... touch you, Mistress?"

Clearly as aroused as I was, her expression softened just a little, and she gave a curt nod. "You may, slave, but only because you've been so good. Don't expect me to let you off this easily all the time."

"I won't, Mistress, I promise."

"Fine. Take off your clothes, then lie on your back. I want to see that stiff cock of yours. And then I'm going to ride it."

I gulped, then hurried to do her bidding. The anticipation, the excitement made me clumsy, and I got my head momentarily stuck in my t-shirt, then became all fingers and thumbs when it came to undoing my jeans and getting them off. Cassie crossed her arms and tapped her foot impatiently. Seconds later I was in the position she'd commanded.

"About damn time, too." She reached down and undid the flap in her leather outfit that gave access to the Heaven between her legs. Then she straddled my stomach, her slickness smearing against my abs. It took every bit of willpower I possessed not to grab her and impale her on my cock.

She crawled up my body and positioned herself over my head. "Lick me. When you've made me come, I'll allow your cock inside me."

"Yes, Mistress." Immediately, I lifted my head to reach her and stuck out my tongue. She hadn't given me permission to use my hands, so I folded them behind my neck for support. The first taste of her tangy sweetness was sublime, and I was sure that if I could see my cock, I'd glimpse the pre-cum seeping from its tip. God, how I wanted her.

I pleasured her the best way I knew how. There was no teasing my Mistress—she wouldn't allow it. So I didn't delay; I went straight for her clit, flicking and circling it with my tongue until it swelled, then sucked it into my mouth and pulled until she came apart.

There was a moment when she stopped being a Mistress, my Mistress, and simply became a woman thrust into oblivion. "Fuck... oh fuck... yes, yes, *yes!*" She continued to swear and babble nonsense as her pleasure washed over her.

I didn't move a muscle. All I wanted was her hot, tight, sheath around my shaft and I wasn't going to do a damn thing to jeopardize that. My good behaviour was rewarded. As soon as she recovered sufficiently, Cassie shifted back down my body, grasped my cock in her hand and pointed it at her entrance. Then, without preamble, she dropped down onto it. One second I was out, the next second, I was in. My body and brain couldn't quite catch up with what was happening, and were further confused when she began to ride me, fast and furious.

I was helpless. All I could do was lie there, almost like some kind of sex machine, rather than a human being. She was fucking me, but using my cock for her own pleasure. I still didn't know if she was going to allow me to come—she'd said I could get inside her, but not that I'd be allowed to climax.

It was torture and perfection all at once. It didn't matter whether she gave me permission to climax or not. My Mistress was on me—in more ways than one—and she was happy. And when she was happy, I was happy.

For me, that was Heaven.

Why I Love Her

I love her for many, many reasons. Because she's my soulmate, because she makes me laugh, because we have fun together.

Most recently, though, I also love her because she said yes. Not "ewww" or "what?!" but a simple, decisive "yes." Her response was so prompt that it made me think that she'd already considered my question at some point, even though I'd never asked it before.

Anal sex had been in the back of my mind for a while, having seen it in porn films, and read about it in the erotic books that Carly has on her bedside table. I'd learned about how pleasurable it could be for both parties, providing there was patience, preparation and lots and lots of lube. Since the information had come from one of Carly's mucky reads, I knew that she knew that, too.

Perhaps that's why she was so up for it. She knew other people got off on it, so why shouldn't we?

I didn't stop to ask any more questions once she'd said yes, fearing she might change her mind. Instead, I leaned towards her on the sofa and kissed her softly on the lips. Then I stood, took her hand in mine and pulled her up, before leading her into the bedroom.

"Now?" she said with a smile, as I shut the door behind us. "You're eager."

I laughed. "You know me, babe. Once a decision's been made, I like to follow through with it as soon as possible. Plus, I got a hard-on as soon as you said yes."

To prove my point, I pressed her hand to my crotch, where my dick strained against the material of my boxers and jeans.

"Well," she replied, rubbing her hand across my cloth-covered erection, which grew harder by the second, "when you put it like that, I guess it'd be rude not to, wouldn't it?"

"It sure would," I replied, giving her a cheeky wink, "now why don't you get naked and comfortable, and I'll grab the things we need."

Carly raised her eyebrows, clearly wondering at my straightforward approach, but she said nothing, merely doing as I asked.

By the time I'd tugged all my own clothes off and grabbed the paraphernalia from a box I'd secreted on the top shelf of my wardrobe, Carly was naked and sprawled on our bed. Her slightly parted legs gave away her arousal; a glint of light reflected from the pussy juices already pooling there.

I moved towards the bed, my stiff dick slapping against my abdomen as I walked. I dropped the goodies onto the duvet then crawled up close to my gorgeous girlfriend, looking forward to some luscious foreplay before the main event. Carly rolled onto her side, reaching out to grab my cock at the same time my hand cupped her left breast. The erect nipple poked into my palm, and my shaft leapt beneath her fingers as we began to pleasure one another.

Our lips met, and we lost ourselves in bliss, enjoying the sensual familiarity even as we anticipated doing something new and kinky together. I moved my hand from her plump tit, stroking down her curvy tummy and down between her legs. My fingers parted her swollen labia and found her cunt wet and willing.

She moaned as I touched her clit. "Ross, make me come, then we'll—"

Her sentence was cut off abruptly as my ministrations on her clit became more focused. I circled the tiny bud of flesh with my fingertips, heartily enjoying Carly's reaction as she writhed on the bed. She tightened her grip on my cock, picking up the pace as I did the same. Soon, I felt my climax waiting in the wings, and had to ask her to stop.

I said, "Let me make you come, babe, and then we'll see what happens next."

She released my cock, then rolled onto her back. Crawling between her legs, I lowered my head to her soaking wet pussy. I sucked in a breath through my nostrils, savouring the scent of her arousal before I tasted it. Naturally, I couldn't wait long. I dipped my tongue between her folds, grinning against the slick flesh as she moaned and sighed.

Clamping my hands onto her thighs to stop her wriggling, I took her clit into my mouth and began to tease it just the way she likes. I sucked, bit and licked at the sensitive bundle of nerve endings until she thrashed beneath me like a wildcat. Then I moved a hand from her thigh and slipped two fingers inside her, curving instantly up to her G-spot. A few seconds of simultaneous stimulation on her clit and G-spot and she was undone.

With a screech, Carly tangled her fingers in my hair and bucked against my face as her orgasm crashed through her body. I sat tight, waiting for her to finish. My cock throbbed. I ached to be inside her red hot, soaking wet pussy, but I knew that I'd also enjoy what we were about to do. And besides, I could always fuck her in the more traditional manner later, if we had enough energy.

"Ross," she said, breathlessly, "get everything ready. I want you now."

Scrambling up from my place between her thighs, I grabbed the stuff I'd dropped onto the bed earlier, double checking I'd got everything we needed. Lube; lots of it. A towel, condoms, cleansing wipes, and of course, the strap-on.

A rush of butterflies fluttered in my stomach as I picked it up. I'd chosen carefully, one with a slim shaft specifically designed for beginners. It had less girth than my cock, and yet when I looked at it and imagined it sliding up my virgin arsehole, I couldn't help but feel a little nervous.

Carly caught sight of me examining the toy, gauging its thickness between my fingers, and gave a gentle smile.

"Babe," she said, plucking it from my grasp, "it will be fine. I know exactly what I'm doing, and we've got all the time in the world. You're going to love it."

She would say that. I'd fucked her up the arse countless times and she fucking loved it. Bounced about on my dick like a woman possessed, in fact. But then I cast my mind back to *her* first time, and how she'd been just as nervous as I was now. We'd taken it super slow, used a ton of lube, and after the initial discomfort for her, it had been incredible.

My nerves dissipated, replaced by resolve. And longing. *I* wanted incredible. I wanted to be fucked up the arse by my incredible girlfriend. More than anything, I wanted to know if it was truly possible for a man to ejaculate during anal sex without any stimulation to his cock. I'd read articles arguing both sides of the case, but I had to know for myself.

I watched wordlessly as Carly slipped off the bed, only to step into the strap-on, secure it around her divine curves and hop back onto the mattress beside me. She knelt up, pointing the flesh coloured silicone dong towards me, then reached down to cradle it in her hand. She touched it as I would my own cock, with firm, confident strokes and even the occasional brush of her thumb across its tip. Of course, by now there would be pre-cum seeping from the tip of a real prick, but it didn't matter. Carly looked comfortable, even cocksure, one might say. Suddenly I wanted nothing more than to have her fake dick inside my arse, fucking me like there was no tomorrow.

It wasn't until I registered the huge grin on her face that I realised I'd said the words out loud.

"As you wish, lover," she responded, giving a couple more rough tugs on her dong. "Get into the position you want, and I'll get us lubed up."

I hesitated for a moment. What position *did* I want? On all fours, so it was easier for Carly to penetrate me, or on my back so we could see each other's faces?

I decided that for my first time, I'd go with the simple option. There would be plenty of time for experimentation later. Grabbing the towel, I shuffled up the bed and knelt on all fours. Shoving the towel between my knees for easy retrieval, I then put my head down close to the pillows, ready to shove one in my mouth to stifle my screams. Just in case.

My ears picked up the sound of squishing, slurping, slicking. Carly was lubing up her cock. More noises, and the sudden chill of her slippery latex-covered fingertips pressing against my hole. I tensed, but forced myself to stay still. The sooner we were both suitably lubricated, the sooner we could fuck ourselves into oblivion. Or Carly could fuck me, anyway. It felt strange, thinking of *her* fucking *me,* instead of the other way around.

Her slim fingers slowly, gently penetrated me. Thanks to the condom, and the copious amount of lube she'd applied, they slid in easily. I did my best to relax; pushing back against the invasion. Allowing her deeper, deeper into my arse, until I felt the tips of her fingers brush against my prostate. I sucked in a breath.

Carly gasped, "Are you all right, babe?"

I nodded emphatically. "I'm fine. You found my prostate. It's gooood."

She giggled. "I did?" Some wriggling in my rear hole. "Oh yeah." She pushed harder, stimulating the protrusion until I fisted my hands into the pillows and begged her to fuck me.

Wordlessly, she removed her fingers. I heard a snap as she removed the condom, then another as she opened the bottle of lube once more, before drizzling a generous amount directly onto my crack. A tiny thump as the bottle was discarded on the duvet. Then, movement behind me as she shuffled closer, closer. Hands on my buttocks, pulling them apart, rotating them, relaxing me. The touch of her cock sliding up and down my perineum, getting the lube spread around everywhere it was needed.

Then, one hand moved from my arse. Milliseconds later I knew she was using it to grip the shaft of the dong, pointing its smooth head towards my entrance. Taking aim. Then she pushed. Slowly, gently, stretching the tight ring of muscle around the strap-on as I held onto the pillows, concentrating on deep breaths to aid my relaxation.

She didn't ask if I was all right. She already knew that my silence held the answer. We'd established a safe word in case I wanted her to stop. I already knew that I wouldn't be using it, and I think she did, too.

A considerable sting as the widest part of the dildo's head pushed past my resistance; then relief, rapidly followed by pleasure. The worst part was undoubtedly over, and the rest of the slim shaft penetrated me with ease, until I felt Carly's rounded tummy pressing against my arse cheeks. She was buried inside me to the hilt.

Gripping my cheeks once more, she gave me a reassuring squeeze. I nodded, then found my voice.

"I'm fine, babe. Just give me one more second, then give me what you've got."

"Okay…"

Pausing momentarily, as I'd asked, Carly then began to move. Slowly at first, she rocked back and forth, exposing tiny increments of her shaft to the outside world before shoving back inside me. My moans and groans clearly reassuring her, she grew more confident. The thrusts became larger, the cock almost all the way out of my tight hole, before being gobbled up once more. Faster, she fucked me, my knuckles turning white with the effort of gripping the pillows, throat quickly growing dry and hoarse with the moans that spilled forth. My eyes were squeezed shut, and I was lost to bliss. The rhythmic caressing, stroking, *pummelling* of my prostate set off a series of reactions in me that I'd never experienced in my life.

Before I had time to assess what they were, what they meant, I felt something else. Much more familiar. A warmth spreading throughout my abdomen and groin, a tingling at the base of my spine, and finally, my balls drawing up closer to my body. In preparation. I was going to come.

I could scarcely believe it. Other than the light foreplay we'd indulged in, my cock hadn't had much stimulation, and yet there I was, hovering on the very edge of an orgasm. And I wanted it more than I'd ever wanted anything.

"Carly," I moaned, pushing back against her, "fuck me harder, I'm going to come."

"Harder?"

"As hard as you can. I promise I'll return the favour later."

She laughed. "Oh, I know you will."

With that, she dug her fingers more tightly into my flesh and picked up her speed. I could sense she was holding back a little, worried about hurting me, but as I rocked back onto the cock, meeting her thrust for thrust, she let go. I heard her sucking in great big breaths, clearly at the limit of physical exertion. But it didn't matter. I was close… so close.

Then, there was the most incredible feeling of release as my cock leapt and twitched beneath me, my balls emptying jet after jet of spunk over the duvet. A spurt even reached as far as the pillow, striping some of my sticky cum across it and one of my hands. I couldn't help it; I laughed. Laughed for the release, laughed with pleasure, bordering on delirium.

With a sigh I dropped my head onto the pillow and scooched forward. Carly took the hint and pulled out of me, just as I flopped down onto the bed. I was vaguely aware of her pulling the towel from where it now lay beneath my thighs. I rolled a little to let her get it, then just lay there on the bed, in a state of something I can't quite describe. It felt like being high. I didn't care. I intended to enjoy it while it lasted.

A few minutes later, Carly crawled up beside me. I reached out and pulled her close, our foreheads touching. Her face was flushed, her eyes gleaming. I suspected I looked pretty much the same.

I kissed her. She slipped an arm around my waist, resting her hand on my buttock. Gave it a cheeky squeeze, then pulled back with a gasp.

"I'm sorry," she said, her hand now resting on my hip, "are you all right?"

"All right?" I said, grabbing her wrist and pushing it back down to its previous position. "Are you kidding? I've never been better!"

She raised her eyebrows. "Oh. I mean, good. I was worried I'd hurt you."

"Did I act like you were hurting me?"

"Well, no—"

I cut her off. "Well then, be quiet. You're ruining my buzz."

She giggled. "Sorry."

"So you should be." I waited a couple of seconds before continuing, the blood refilling my cock spurring me on to utter my next words. "So… about me returning the favour."

"Mmm?"

"Assume the position, sweetie, and I'll get the lube."

"Yes, Sir!"

Good god, but I love her. For many, many, reasons. But mainly because she says yes.

At the Car Wash

Harriet considered her outfit carefully. She needed access, and she needed it fast. Also, she had to be able to hide what she was doing; she wanted a cheap, exciting thrill, not a warrant for her arrest and a restraining order.

After some deliberation, she chose a form-fitting black top that never failed to make her feel sexy, and a loose, floaty knee-length skirt, also in black. Granted, she'd put together a dark-coloured outfit which would absorb heat to wear on one of the hottest days of the year, but she'd be fine. Thankfully she had air-conditioning in the car. Plus, the very idea of what she was about to do was already making her feel all hot and bothered, so it wouldn't make much difference.

What really mattered, after all, was what *they* would be wearing. Or, more accurately, what they *wouldn't* be wearing. Harriet had deliberately not cleaned her car for ages, then chosen a day with record temperatures to take it to the hand car wash. Why?

Because being called boring by the man she'd thought was the love of her life had been a slap in the face. More of a punch, really. Especially when she'd come to the conclusion that he was right. Now she lived for danger and naughty sexual escapades. A visit to the hand car wash where several shirtless, muscular men would clean her car while she sat inside with her hand down her knickers was definitely in order. It had been on her dirty bucket list for some time and having already ticked off several other items, it was time to give the car wash fantasy a try.

Harriet dressed carefully, then tied her hair up into a high ponytail and applied a fresh coat of makeup. She wasn't trying to impress anyone, but the more attractive she felt, the more likely she'd be to come before she got caught.

Grabbing her purse and car keys, she headed out to her car and got in. She started the engine and pulled on her seatbelt. Just before reversing off the drive, though, she looked around, noting the position of her seat in relation to all the windows. Harriet figured that the only way they'd be able to see what she was doing – and even then they probably wouldn't believe it – was if they were looking through the passenger side window. She was so close to the driver's side window that the angle was all wrong.

Nodding to herself, Harriet put the car in gear, released the handbrake and manoeuvred off the drive on the way to her illicit adventure. The hand car wash was only a five minute drive away, but she was so excited that she could barely wait to get there. As a result, she broke out in a light sweat and a wash of heat rose up her cheeks and gathered between her legs. Huffing, Harriet switched on the air conditioning, then grinned. If she was already feeling this agitated and horny, she'd probably end up coming before they'd even given her car a preliminary once over with the jet spray. She might even manage two orgasms.

Harriet shook her head as she pulled into the hand car wash. She knew that wasn't possible, really. There'd be no time for thinking, for hesitation. And, due to the lack of any other patrons – she'd picked her arrival time carefully and it had paid off - her time was now. Right. Fucking. Now.

Beaming as the topless guy approached her car, Harriet wound down the window and told him she just wanted the outside of the car cleaning. Truthfully, the inside could have done with it too, but there was no way she was going to fling the door open and get out having just masturbated in her car while they washed it. It was unlikely her legs would hold her up, in any case.

No, she'd stay safely ensconced in her little motor –

Her thought process was interrupted by much waving from the several men standing a couple of dozen feet away. They were ready and beckoning her into position. All except one were shirtless, and he wore a tank top, so she still had a delicious view of his arms, which were definitely worth looking at.

After winding the window back up, she inched closer until one man held up a hand indicating she should stop. Harriet did so immediately, and simultaneously slipped a hand up her skirt, shoved her barely-there thong to one side and stroked her fingers through her folds. Her pussy was already damp, and as she gazed out of the window at the half-naked men surrounding her car, she began to play. Cautiously, at first, but as the spray of the jet wash caused her car to rock and vibrate – not to mention obscuring the windows – Harriet grew braver and more enthusiastic.

Knowing the additional movement she was causing inside the car would go unnoticed, Harriet rubbed her clit vigorously, occasionally dipping down between her pussy lips for more juices to slick over her swollen nub. Part of her wanted to close her eyes, but she didn't. Instead, her gaze flicked from the windscreen, to the side mirrors and windows, to the rear view mirror in turn, checking out the flexing muscles that were alternately spraying, rubbing and buffing her car. They were a sight to behold, and had one pulled her out of the car and bent her over it, she wouldn't have resisted. Not even if they'd passed her round like the last cigarette.

Soon, she couldn't see through the windows at all. The gorgeous half-naked guys had soaped up every inch of the bodywork and glass, adding another—albeit temporary—screen between them. For now, Harriet had to let her imagination pick up the slack, pulling up mental images of the men that were inches away, busily squirting, scrubbing and spraying her car. If anything, her imagined images were even sexier than the ones she'd physically seen.

She picked up the pace between her legs as her mind provided extra stimulation, thoughts of what those damp, soapy hands would feel like on her flesh.

Boy was it hot. As Harriet's right hand continued to stroke and pinch at her clit, her left flicked the air conditioning switch, lowering the temperature even further, as she was in danger of spontaneously combusting. A fresh blast of cold air was a blessing over her heated skin, making her aware of the fact that clean water was now being aimed at her car. They'd almost finished washing; she'd soon have to move the car around the corner to the area where they dried and polished, and cleaned the windows.

Harriet had literally seconds to go. Milliseconds perhaps. Concentrating fully on the pleasant rock and rumble of her car, and the damp fingers manipulating her clit, Harriet bit her lip as she felt the welcome wave of orgasm wash over her. She couldn't help it – her eyes squeezed closed and she let out an involuntary squeak as her legs clamped together over her hand. Her pussy clenched forcefully, the strength of the climax taking Harriet's breath away and leaving her feeling like a mass of quivering jelly. Thank god she was sitting down.

A bang brought her back to earth with a bump. The guy in the tank top had tapped on the bonnet of her car, bringing her attention to the guys waving madly and indicating she should move on. Snatching her hand from her crotch and yanking her skirt down, she put the car in gear and drove around to the drying area, her pussy fluttering the whole time. Her heart thudded in her chest. That had been seriously fucking close.

Not to mention seriously fucking good. A grin spread across Harriet's face as it dawned on her that she'd done it. She'd crossed another item off her dirty bucket list. A cheeky wank in a hand car wash without getting caught.

As the muscular men surrounded her car once more, buffing and spraying various chemicals on the windows, tyres, trims and paintwork, Harriet adopted a happy, relaxed expression. She had plenty of time to leap around and congratulate herself when she got home, but she'd just have to keep her excitement at her dirty little secret under wraps for a little longer.

Finally, when her car was shining and sparkly clean and she handed over the cash to pay, she caught the eye of one of the other guys. He was watching her with an expression akin to hunger, then when he realised she was looking back at him, his face broke into a knowing grin and he gave her a lusty wink.

Taking her change with a hasty word of thanks, Harriet wound up the window and drove out of the hand car wash as fast as was safely possible.

Perhaps her dirty little secret hadn't been so secret after all...

Nevertheless, it had been worth it. Harriet had left boring well and truly behind her, and was having the most exciting, sexy time of her life.

She could hardly wait to check out her bucket list and see what was next.

The Not-So-Blushing Bride

I never, not once, ever thought that it would actually happen. Until it did.

And now I can't get it out of my mind.

I'm a chauffeur, and the majority of my work is driving wedding cars. You know, taking the bride and her wedding party to church. Then taking the newlyweds to their wedding reception and sometimes, later, onto the airport or a hotel.

So you can hardly blame me for having weddings on the brain. As a bloke, though, it's not the wedding itself that I think about. I don't get all gooey and gushy over the church, the dress, the rings, the flowers, the cake. That would be weird.

It's the bride that occupies my thoughts. Now, before you think I'm some kind of creepy pervert, let me explain. It's not like that. I don't paw at the brides that ride in my car, flirt, or make inappropriate comments. In fact, I don't do anything that would make them uncomfortable. I am the epitome of professionalism and respectability at all times.

Until they get out of the car and go on their way, that is. It's the times that I'm left to my own devices that my mind starts to wander down its naughty path. And, given that I'm generally employed for entire days with long periods of time where I do nothing but sit around, you can hardly blame me for doing something to occupy my time.

So I entertain myself by sitting in the car. It's not as boring as you might think. I have an eReader, therefore I have plenty of reading material at my fingertips, and if I'm hungry or thirsty, I can jump into the back of the limo and grab something that the company has supplied for the wedding party. Naturally, I don't sample any alcohol – I'm not an idiot.

I don't think dirty thoughts every time I'm sat alone in the limousine; despite the statistics, men don't think of sex constantly. A lot, yes, but not *constantly*. Usually, it depends on the bride. If I don't find her attractive, then I tend to do lots of reading in my periods of downtime. However, if she's hot then my imagination fires on all cylinders.

Which brings me neatly back to my fantasy. You know, the one that recently came true, in spectacular style. So, here goes:

I have always wanted to fuck a bride on her way to her wedding.

Despite knowing that the majority of brides these days aren't exactly pure and innocent, I've always really fancied screwing one of them senseless in the back of my limo before dropping them off at their destination, where they'll commit themselves to someone else for the rest of their lives. There's no need to start psychoanalysing it – I know it's because it's taboo, forbidden, corrupt. And therein lies the attraction. And, as I said, for a long time it was just a harmless fantasy that nobody knew about.

Then Daisy came along.

Usually, the bride is accompanied from her house – or wherever she got ready for her wedding – with at least one other person. This, naturally, has always made my fantasy completely unattainable. I could hardly see the father of the bride turning a blind eye while the hired help lifts up his little girl's dress and fucks her, could you?

Daisy bucked the trend – in more ways than one.

First, she was ready when I knocked on the door. Usually I turn up a little early in order to spur preparations on a little. I know brides are meant to be fashionably late – but often, if it weren't for me, they'd be pushing-their-luck-late.

Second, she looked nothing like a bride. When Daisy answered the door, I looked past her into the hallway, about to ask where the bride was, when she pulled the door shut behind her and said, "Shall we?"

I promptly shut my mouth and held out my arm to escort her to the car. All the while, I was discreetly checking her out. I'd seen a lot of different wedding dresses in my years as a chauffeur, but Daisy managed to surprise even me. For starters, I'd never seen a bride wear black before. She looked like a Goth, particularly with the crazy purple stripe in her black hair, heavy makeup and platform boots.

Third, she wasn't remotely nervous. She was full of happy chatter from the moment she walked out her front door, even asking me to open the partition between the cab and the rear of the limo so we could talk on the way to the registry office. I didn't mind – it certainly made my job more pleasant and besides, she was really interesting to talk to.

Not to mention completely gorgeous. She may not have

looked like a typical bride, but she was still stunning. Even as we were yakking nineteen-to-the-dozen, I was imagining what she was wearing under that slinky dress.

As it happened, though, I wasn't the only one with sex on the brain. When she first gave me directions to somewhere other than the registry office, I didn't think anything of it. I just thought perhaps her nerves were finally kicking in and she needed a little breathing space.

As I followed her next command, I asked, "Everything all right?"

"Oh yes, Bradley. Everything is just fine."

I shrugged and carried on driving. It was only when she directed me down a quiet country lane that I finally started to think that something wasn't right. My overactive imagination began to wonder if I'd been duped – perhaps Daisy was part of a gang, and they were going to knock me out, leave me for dead and make off with the limo.

As I plotted how I was going to get out of the predicament, Daisy spoke again. "Bradley, pull over in that lay by, then get in the back."

Something about her tone made me relax – I wasn't about to be carjacked. As the tension seeped out of me, the arousal crept in. Why did she want me to get into the back of the car? She couldn't possibly want to...

"Take off your hat and jacket. And put the screen back up so nobody can see us."

Despite my brain's misgivings, the blood rushed to my cock. It was all I could do to park the car without crashing.

As soon as I shut the door, Daisy made her intentions blatant. "Get your cock out, Bradley. We don't have long."

"But... won't we be more than fashionably late?"

"Not if you're quick. I deliberately booked the car fifteen minutes early. I've always wanted to fuck a chauffeur."

There was no arguing with that. I grappled with my belt and fly, and pulled out my cock. Daisy's green eyes glinted as she passed me the condom she'd just retrieved from her cleavage. Without a word, I ripped open the packaging and rolled the rubber on. When I looked back up, Daisy was already kneeling on the floor of the limo, the top half of her body leaning on the seats and with her dress up around her back. She wore a tiny black thong.

I knew this was no time for hesitation. I'd fantasised about fucking a bride, she'd fantasised about fucking a chauffeur. It was a win-win situation.

I pulled her thong to one side, grabbed her hips and positioned my cock at her entrance. She was already wet, so when she pushed back, I slid in effortlessly. I paused, savouring the sensation.

"Bradley, we don't have much time."

I didn't need telling twice. Gripping Daisy's pert arse, I fucked her, hard and fast. The sensation of her pussy was divine; hot, wet and tight, and it wasn't long before the feel of it, coupled with the riskiness of the entire situation, pushed me to the edge.

"Daisy..." I said, warningly.

"It's okay... I am too."

Then, my orgasm hit with force. I let out a violent shout as my balls emptied into the not-exactly-blushing bride, who was clearly in the throes of her own climax. We yelled and moaned together in pleasure, before calming down, then disentangling without a word. I snapped off the condom and threw it into the bin.

"You know how to get to the registry office from here?" Daisy asked.

I nodded, tucked myself away, then clambered out of the car and back into the driver's seat. I pulled on my hat and jacket and straightened myself up before starting the engine and driving to the original destination. I didn't open the partition again until we pulled up outside the building.

"Ready?"

She nodded, and I resumed my professional persona as I helped her out of the car.

"Okay from here?"

Daisy nodded, and gave me a cheeky wink before heading inside. Just before she was swallowed into the gloom of the building's hallway, I spotted a suspicious-looking stain on the back of her dress.

I didn't say anything. It wasn't my place.

Clipped

Nancy fidgeted and messed around with the things on her desk as she waited for her documents to print. All fifty pages of it—twice over. No wonder it was taking forever. She'd finished her to-do list for the day and the document was literally her last task, bar separating the two copies, keeping one for herself and stuffing the other in an envelope and dashing to the post box just outside her building. The address and postage labels were ready to go, too.

God, it really was taking an age. She could almost feel herself getting older as she waited. Irritably, she flipped the lid off the small plastic box holding her paperclips and emptied them out onto the desk. She was so bored that she started sorting them into piles based on their colour; red, blue, green, pink. She quickly grew fed up of that game and began linking the clips together. Slipping one onto another and making a chain. It wasn't challenging, or even particularly interesting, but somehow it lulled Nancy into a kind of trance, and the end of the row of paperclips soon reached the floor. She carried on putting them together as the printer churned away in the background.

"Er, Nance, what are you doing?"

Gerard's voice came out of the blue, startling her. She dropped her crazy creation and pressed a hand to her pounding heart. "Fuck, Ger, I didn't hear you come in."

"Obviously not," he said, nodding towards the brightly-coloured pile on the floor and smirking at her. "Having fun, were we, babe?"

She flicked him the 'V' sign. "I was just bored, that's all," she said, bending to pick up the paperclips. "This document is taking forever to print, and I have nothing else to do while I'm waiting."

"I have an idea," Gerard said, walking across their open-plan flat and standing beside Nancy's chair. "How about," he grabbed an arm of the chair and swivelled it so she was facing him, "we have some fun?" He leaned down to kiss her, grinning as a soft moan escaped her lips.

Nancy twisted her head away. "You know what, I like the sound of that. Shall we move over to the bed?"

"God, no," he replied, "I think we should take advantage of where you are right now." He straightened, then grabbed the chain of paperclips from her hand. "And I think these might come in handy, too."

"Why, what are you going to do? Clip me to the chair?"

"Yes, that's exactly what I'm going to do." He held each end of the row and stretched it out to its full length. "Wow, you were bored, weren't you babe? Just as well, too, because I'm definitely going to put this to good use. Hold on to the arms of the chair, please."

Nancy frowned, then reluctantly did as Gerard said. Immediately he looped the chain around one of her wrists, fiddling and manipulating to create a makeshift handcuff, then did the same with her other arm. So she was pinned to the chair with sort of-handcuffs, and the handcuffs were connected by a row of paperclips. It looked bizarre; it *was* bizarre, but somehow, the situation took the arousal inflicted by Gerard's kiss and multiplied it. The warmth between her legs grew hotter, and as her husband leaned down to capture her lips with his once more, blood rushed to her crotch and her labia and clit began to swell.

By the time he pulled away, she was gasping, her heart racing, and her clit and pussy ached. Everything except for her and Gerard had faded into the background, including the insistent chugging of the printer.

"Horny, baby?" he said, quirking an eyebrow.

She nodded enthusiastically.

He reached down, pressed a hand to the crotch of his jeans and rearranged himself. "Just as well, really, because I am, too. I'm also very happy that you're wearing a skirt. That makes my job much easier."

"Y—your job?" He looked so intense—and damn sexy—that her brain short-circuited and she couldn't grasp what he was talking about.

"Yes," he said, dropping to his knees in front of the chair, "my job. Now stop talking."

She gripped the arms of the chair tightly as she finally realised what Gerard meant. He pressed his knees to the base of the chair to stop it moving, then reached forwards and grabbed her buttocks, pulling her to the edge of the seat. He then flipped up her skirt, roughly tugged the gusset of her thong to one side and let out a low growl as he feasted his gaze upon her splayed pussy.

"God, you're so wet already, Nance. I can't wait to make you come and lick up every drop that leaks out of your delicious cunt."

He hadn't even touched her there yet, but his words, so rude and so honest, made her groan and wriggle, and she fancied that her entrance was gaping, so eager was she to feel him inside her. His fingers, his cock, whatever. She just wanted him, and soon.

A light slap on her thigh made her squeal. "Keep still, otherwise I'll get some more paperclips and wrap them around your damn legs and waist."

"S—sorry." She wasn't too worried about his threat—after all, how tough could paperclips be? They weren't exactly a silk scarf, deceptively tough, or thick leather handcuffs, were they?

As soon as Gerard shifted his attention back to her pussy, she surreptitiously tried to move her arm. Fuck, it was held fast. She tugged harder, watching as the clips stretched and bent slightly, but then did nothing more but make crazy white patterns on her skin with the pressure. On some parts of her wrists, the exposed ends of the clips dug sharply into her skin. If she carried on, she'd leave herself with weird scratches, and people would think she'd been self-harming or something. She stopped testing their strength; it was pointless. They certainly wouldn't bend enough for her to escape. Not that she really wanted to, she'd just been curious, and now her curiosity had abated.

It flew out of the window altogether when Gerard's hot mouth touched her vulva. Her swollen lips, already totally slick with her juices, welcomed his touch and she resisted the temptation to jerk her hips forward, forcing her harder onto him. She knew if she did, she'd somehow pay for it—and not in a good way—so she pulled in a shaky breath and kept perfectly still.

She was rewarded when Gerard slowly pushed his tongue between her fattened labia and wriggled it around. He did this for a few seconds, which produced an almost ticklish sensation, then changed tactics and began to sweep his tongue from just above her anus to the very tip of her clitoris, over and over, at a maddeningly slow pace. It felt good, but nowhere near good enough to make her climax, or even set her on the journey. It was pleasant, rather than arousing, and she suspected that Gerard knew that, and was doing it on purpose. God knows he'd gone down on her enough times in the years they'd been together and he knew exactly what got her going.

He hummed, sending a delicious jolt through her and a fresh gush of juices trickling from her sex. He lapped them all up quickly and eagerly, then upped his game. Curling up the edges of his tongue, he began to fuck her with it, stimulating all the most sensitive nerve endings at her entrance and making her grip the chair so hard that her knuckles went white and she closed her eyes, lolling her head back. Normally, at this point, she'd have tangled her fingers into his thick blond hair and pulled him more tightly to her cunt, urging him on, showing him just how much she wanted to come, but obviously she couldn't. The paperclip bondage prevented that.

After teasing her until she was dizzy, Gerard did what he knew would put her on the fast track to orgasm. He concentrated wholly on her clit. He circled it, he flicked his tongue up and down across it, then from side to side, tantalising every nerve ending in the tiny nub. He did this until she was wailing so much the neighbours probably thought she was being tortured, then he pulled the sensitive bud into his mouth and sucked, gently at first, then harder and harder until he had to push Nancy's thighs down to stop her kicking.

"Oh, Ger… I'm going to come!" she moaned.

He popped his mouth from her, making her growl with frustration. "That's kind of the point, sweetheart. Now shut up and hang on tight."

"As if I've got a fucking choice." She shook her hands, showing just how effective her bonds were.

Her irritation quickly dissipated when Gerard continued what he'd been doing, pulling her clit back into his mouth and sucking and tonguing it. The longer he did it, the faster and harder he went, pushing her higher and higher until the perfect sensation of pre-climax took over her body. Her abdomen tightened, as if a spring were being wound inside it, tighter and tighter still, until she was overtaken by something that felt like sparks, making all the hairs on her skin stand on end. Finally, the sparks ignited and she came, the spring released, her cunt spasmed wildly and hot juices squirted from her sex and onto Gerard's waiting tongue. She squealed.

After a minute or two, she slowly returned to earth, gradually aware that Gerard was no longer touching her. She opened her eyes and saw him, crouched in front of her, watching her with an expression that looked like awe.

"Fucking hell, babe, that was amazing," she said, her tongue feeling thick in her mouth. "I came so hard it almost hurt."

Her husband grinned. "I aim to please, sweetheart. I can see I'll have to tie you up with paperclips more often. Perhaps the next time you're printing an epic document, you could start making some more of those chains. I'll put them in the toy box." He jumped back to avoid her swinging foot, then shot out a hand and grabbed her ankle, pulling the chair—and of course, Nancy—towards him. He bent and kissed her once more, and she could taste her own sweet and tangy juices on his lips, and feel his still-hard cock pressing against her through his jeans.

"Actually," she said, rocking her hips to hint at what she'd like to do next, "that's not such a bad idea. I'll put it on my to-do list. Now, let me out of these damn… paperclips, and I'll see about returning the favour. God, doesn't that sound ridiculous? Let me out of these damn paperclips. Ha!"

Gerard didn't reply, instead tackling the tangle of coloured plastic clips to release her. Once she was freed, he pulled her into his arms and sat back. They rolled on the floor together, the bizarre bondage forgotten. They were so lost in one another, lost in lust, that they didn't even notice the document had finished printing. And if they had, they wouldn't have cared.

When He Gets Home

As soon as Nina heard the rumble of her husband's car engine as it pulled onto the drive, she dropped her book and all but leapt out of her chair. Moving fast across the living room, then through the kitchen, she flung open the internal door which led into the garage. Walking in, she closed it behind her. Standing, arms folded, one foot tapping repeatedly on the floor, she waited for Owen to drive the car into the garage, then press the button which shut the door behind him and the vehicle. When the bottom of the up-and-over touched concrete and the car's ignition was shut off, she practically ran around to the driver's side and tugged the door open before Owen got the chance.

The sight of his wife standing there, an indeterminable expression on her face, made Owen's heart sink. He had no idea what was going on, and she never normally came into the garage to meet him when he got home. She didn't look very happy. He didn't speak, as he suspected whatever he said would be the wrong thing.

Nina didn't speak, either. There were no words to explain what she was thinking and feeling right now, so she decided that instead of talking, she'd just act. She leaned forward and touched the button to drop the back of the seat Owen was sitting in, smirking at his expression—the poor man had no idea what was coming to him. She was going to make sure he'd never forget it.

Owen's body jerked as he responded to the shock of the back support disappearing from behind him. Nina's expression still looked strange—yet eerily beautiful—and when she rested a palm on his chest and shoved him, he landed on the now-flat backrest with a thump which knocked the air out of his lungs. "W—what are you—" His hastily spoken words were cut off when Nina straddled his lap and silenced him by leaning down and pressing her lips to his.

Nina couldn't help but find Owen's reaction amusing. He looked as though he thought she was going to kill him, or something. Despite that, she felt his cock hardening beneath her and was glad her husband's body was ready, even if his brain couldn't quite catch up. She knelt up enough so she could slide her hand between their bodies and cup his crotch, squeezing and stroking his rapidly growing erection.

Owen's eyes widened as his wife played with his hard on

through his suit trousers, then abruptly tugged down his fly, slipped her hand through the gap and manoeuvred his cock out through it. Part of him wanted to say something about the fact the edges of the zip might scratch his shaft, possibly even draw blood, but the rest of him told him to shut up complaining—he was about to get laid. In the car, no less!

Enjoying the feeling of warm velvet over a core of steel in her hand, Nina wrapped her fingers more tightly around Owen's cock and began to stroke it slowly, ensuring he was fully erect before moving so her hips rested over his. She tucked the material of her skirt to one side, revealing her knicker-less lady parts. Then, aiming the head of his prick at her entrance, she slowly lowered herself onto him, her damp pussy growing rapidly wetter at the excitement and danger of what they were doing.

Owen let out a moan as the wet warmth of his wife's cunt sunk down onto his cock. The saucy wench had come out here with no knickers on, set on seducing him! She clapped her hand over his mouth quickly, muffling the sound. She put a finger of her other hand to her lips, then pointed upwards. *Ahh, the kids were in.* He nodded in understanding, and she released him.

Wordlessly, Nina began to bounce up and down on his dick, lifting herself so he almost popped out of her, just the very tip of him inside, then dropped down heavily. It wasn't a particularly fast movement, but it was packed full of friction and she knew that if she carried on like that, it wouldn't be long before Owen shot his load. Desperate to ensure she got her rocks off, too, she grabbed one of his hands from around her waist and thrust it to her crotch. Mercifully, he got the hint and, gathering some juices from where their bodies joined, he smeared them over her swollen clit and started to stroke.

Owen's actions had a knock-on effect. Touching his wife's nub caused her eyes to roll back in her head and her pussy to contract around his cock, which in turn made his cock to throb and twitch inside her. He'd have to up his game if he wanted to make sure she came before—or at the same time as—him. Grasping the slippery and sensitive bundle of nerve endings between his finger and thumb, he rolled and pinched at it. Amazingly, it swelled further at his ministrations, and he looked up to see Nina stifling her own moans by biting down on her fist.

Nina knew it wouldn't be long now, for either of them. The setting and situation were unusual, forbidden, quite kinky, particularly for her and her husband. She was sure other couples had sex in all kinds of weird and wonderful places, but she and Owen were very much missionary-in-bed kind of people. Judging by the way they were both reacting to the impromptu fuck in the garage, though, that was set to change. Her pussy fluttered around Owen's shaft, and the tightening in her abdomen, like a spring wound tighter and tighter, told her just how imminent her climax was. "You close?"

Owen nodded, glad that Nina was almost ready to come, as he knew there was no way he could hold on for much longer. He wished he could see her gorgeous body as she bounced up and down on his shaft, her perfect tits and arse, her curves in all the right places... but it wasn't the time or the place. Maybe later. Right now, though, the tingle at the base of his spine and the tightening of his balls told him he was approaching the point of no return. He stimulated Nina's clit faster and harder, seeking that particular spot which never failed to send her over the edge. The twitches around his shaft and her heavy breathing indicated he'd found it. He focussed hard on it as Nina rode them both to completion.

Nina dug her teeth harder into her hand, her eyes widening as Owen manipulated the most sensitive spot, just at the edge of her clitoral hood. He knew it drove her crazy, and clearly intended to take advantage of that fact. Soon, the sensation of her abdomen was at breaking point and she removed her fingers from her mouth just in time to whisper, "Now."

Owen let go, the spunk making its journey from his balls, up his shaft and out of his slit in what seemed like record time. He gripped Nina's hips hard—harder than he meant to—and squeezed his eyes and mouth closed in an attempt not to shout out as the intense sensations of climax crashed through every last cell of his body. He couldn't prevent the odd humming noise he made, but nobody but Nina would have been able to hear it in any case.

Nina slumped down onto Owen's prone form, her cunt still twitching wildly around his shaft as she rode out the waves of her pleasure. They smashed into her, again and again, wringing her out, turning her world upside down in the most perfect, blissful way. It seemed like an age since she'd had an orgasm like that, and she suspected that come bedtime, she'd be eager for another one.

They lay panting together for a few moments more, until Owen cupped his wife's face in his hands and gave her a long, lingering kiss. He pulled away earlier than he really wanted to, aware that if he carried on much longer, they'd both end up ready and raring to go again, and they were already running the risk of being caught. "Baby," he said, stroking Nina's hair, "as much as I'd love to lie here all night with you, and definitely fuck you again, do you think we ought to go inside?"

Nina sighed. "I suppose so. Ugh."

They reluctantly made themselves decent, clambered out of the car and headed into the house. Owen, more out habit than any need for security, pressed the button on his key fob to lock the door, before closing the door to the garage.

"So," Nina said as innocently as possible to her husband, having spotted the kids entering the kitchen, "how was your trip, darling? Glad to have you home."

"It was fine, sweetheart, thank you. But I couldn't have wished for a better homecoming. Hi, kids!"

After the Party

Lisa giggled as she watched the varying expressions on her friends' faces as they passed the vibrator around. The bubbly representative running the party was a friend of a friend, and had switched the toy on before passing it to the woman nearest her, instructing them all to have a go at holding it to the tips of their noses to get an idea of its power.

There were shrieks, gasps and oohs as each woman took her turn. Nudges, winks and laughs followed, as they decided whether or not to add the buzzing thing to their list of orders.

It was the first time Lisa had been to one of these events. They consisted of a bunch of female friends, and an employee of the popular sex toy and underwear company, who would pass around various sex toys, books, underwear and more, so they could all look at them without fear or recrimination, before passing them on. Wine was consumed, silly games were played—put a condom on a banana with your mouth, anyone?—and, most importantly, the orders were taken in confidence before the evening was over. If someone wanted to divulge what they'd purchased, then that was fine. But delivery was made in sealed bags to the party host's home for the others to pick up. So if someone wanted to keep their purchases secret, they could.

Lisa swallowed her wine, as Francesca—or Frankie as she was more commonly known—passed her the toy. She already had a rabbit vibrator, but she didn't particularly want to share that information—she hadn't imbibed nearly enough alcohol for that yet—and so she played along, ooh-ing as the garish pink sex toy vibrated hard on her nose. It was powerful, but no more so than the one she already had, so she handed it to her neighbour with a grin, instantly dismissing it and continuing to leaf through the catalogue on her lap.

She hadn't come to the party with the express intention of buying anything. Really, she'd just agreed because Frankie had told her they were a good laugh. And she was always game for a giggle.

Lisa and her husband Dean had a fun and varied sex life, without any particular need for toys, but she'd kept an open mind and decided that if she saw something she wanted to try, she'd buy it. If not, then maybe she'd splash out on some sexy underwear. She had loads already, but Dean sure seemed to appreciate the lacy bras, frilly knickers, baby dolls and stockings she occasionally paraded around in. And it was worth every last penny to see the lust in his hooded eyes as he regarded her, then threw her onto the bed, floor or sofa—whatever was nearest—and had his wicked and delicious way with her.

As the time ticked on and everyone became louder and drunker, the rep started pulling out the more risqué items. Peephole bras, crotchless knickers, PVC clothes, handcuffs, whips and the like. The giggles became gasps and full-on belly laughs as the group examined the kinky items, poking their fingers through the various holes, held the skimpy garments up against their bodies and slapped items of punishment against their palms.

By this point, the alcohol Lisa had drunk had created a pleasant buzz throughout her bloodstream and she felt much more relaxed, not to mention daring. She sauntered around the room with a PVC dress clasped to her, resulting in raucous laughter from the other women. By the time she flopped back into her seat, Frankie was tapping her own palm with a leather spanking paddle, growing gradually more forceful.

"Ooh," Lisa said, leaning in closer to her friend, "does it hurt?"

"A little, but it's not unbearable. And I'm not doing it that hard. Want me to try it on you?"

Lisa nodded, then, before she really knew what she was doing, she'd stood up and turned around, presenting her arse to her friend. "Spank me, baby!"

Frankie was disbelieving. "Are you sure? I meant on your hand!"

"Yeah, I know. But I've got a big arse, I can take it."

"You have not! But okay, if you say so."

With that, Lisa waited a second or two, trying not to tense her buttocks as she waited for the inevitable blow. The room fell silent as everyone else realised what was going on and turned to watch.

Then it came. The thick leather slapped squarely across both her arse cheeks, leaving a stinging blow in their wake, even through the denim of her jeans. The noise made it appear worse than it was, but the shock—and, if she admitted it only to herself, her audience—caused her to jolt upright with a shriek and clutch her bottom.

Spinning around, she directed her words at Frankie. "Ow!"

she said, rubbing the affronted flesh. "You didn't break me in bloody gently, did you? That fucking hurt."

Frankie looked apologetic. "Sorry," she replied, quickly leaning across to pass the object in question to the next person in the group. "I didn't do it on purpose. It must hurt more the further away you are from the smackee, I suppose. I'm really sorry. Here, have some more wine." She grabbed the bottle that was down by her feet, unscrewed the lid and splashed liquid into Lisa's glass until it was almost full.

"Thanks," Lisa said grumpily, slowly sitting back down, still wincing a little from the residual pain. Accepting the glass from her friend, she gave her a slightly watery grin and took a big gulp. Thankfully, everyone seemed to have moved on now, and the party rep continued pulling things out of her suitcase to interest and titillate her potential clients. Lisa was pleased the focus was off her, and not just because she didn't like being stared at. The truth was, she'd liked it when Frankie had paddled her bum. Yes, it had been shocking, had stung and now left a dull ache behind, but it had also translated into not a small amount of arousal. Blood had coursed through her veins and pooled in her groin, causing her labia and clitoris to swell.

Shifting in her seat, she pressed her thighs together, trying to either gain some kind of satisfaction, or encourage the arousal to go away—she wasn't sure which.

She barely noticed the next bunch of items that got passed around. Sure, she engaged and played with each thing, as was expected, but nothing really sunk in, or struck a note. All she could think about was the continuing ache between her legs and the spank on the arse that had caused it.

Finally, she resolved to do something about it. Not right then—she may have been a tiny little bit drunk, but there was no way she was going to sneak out and stroke herself to orgasm. No, she'd wait, and do it right. And that meant getting Dean involved. She'd buy the spanking paddle, and probably a few other bits and pieces so it didn't look so conspicuous, so significant, and ask Dean if he'd like to try something a little different. They'd experimented with lots of things, including tying up and blindfolding, but not spanking or other forms of corporal punishment. The throbbing in her groin told her it was long overdue. She was going to count the seconds until she owned her very own spanking paddle and get her husband to redden her arse with it. Already she could hardly wait. She'd have to, of course, but in the meantime, Dean would be getting some damn good sex, and plenty of it.

When Frankie popped to the toilet, Lisa took advantage of the relative privacy and flicked hurriedly to the catalogue page that held the coveted item and noted down its name, product number and price on her form. She glanced to her other side—Helen wasn't taking the slightest bit of notice, thankfully, so she flicked back to a more innocent page and continued to browse.

By the time the party was over, she'd added several more items to her list, and waited as the rep called each of them in turn to give her their orders and pay what was owed. A sign of the times was the portable credit card machine the woman had. Lisa slotted her card into the device, putting in her pin when prompted, then taking her card and receipt, stifling a grin as she headed back into the host's living room. She could hear everybody asking their neighbours what they'd bought, or what they intended to buy, and one glance at her friend told Lisa that Frankie would be no exception. Thankfully, she had an answer ready, and it wasn't a lie. Not completely, anyway.

"So," Frankie said, beaming, "what have you bought?"

"I'll tell you mine if you tell me yours."

Frankie nodded in agreement. "Okay."

"Okay. I've had a couple of those erotic books, a sexy underwear set and some hold-up stockings."

Her friend narrowed her eyes. "Is that all? You haven't bought one of those rabbit vibrators then? I saw your reaction when you put it on the tip of your nose!"

"Nope," Lisa replied firmly. "I've already got one, why would I need another?"

"What!" Frankie yelled, drawing the attention of the other women in the room. "You kept that one fucking quiet, didn't you? Already got a bloody rabbit vibrator and didn't tell me."

"I don't have to tell you everything, do I? It's private, in any case. I don't ask for all the details of your sex life—you just tell me anyway."

Frankie cackled. "That's true. I guess I'm just more open than you. In more ways than one." She continued to laugh, and by the time her mirth abated, she had tears running down her cheeks. "Come on, babe, let's ring a taxi. I think I've had enough."

The time it took Jeanette—the party's host—to phone and let her know the rep had dropped off the orders felt like an age. Though she'd filled some of that time by making love to her husband on a nightly basis, much to both of their delights.

"Come and pick it up whenever you like," Jeanette said.

"Okay," Lisa replied, "are you in now? I'm just on my way back from town, I could swing by on the way home. If that's all right?"

"No problem. I'll see you in a few."

She wanted to drive faster, because the sooner she got to Jeanette's, the sooner she could make her excuses and go home. But she refused to break the speed limit, so she got there in approximately fifteen minutes and pasted a smile on her face before ringing the doorbell.

"Hi!" Jeanette said, a little too enthusiastically in Lisa's opinion. Perhaps she'd bought some of those jiggle ball thingies, and had slipped them in before making the phone calls. The thought both amused and disturbed her.

"Hello," she replied, stepping into the hallway. "How are you?"

"Good, thanks. You know, busy as always, with the business, the kids, the husband. It was quite nice to be forced to take a break when the rep turned up with the parcels. Can you stay for a coffee? Or tea?"

"Umm..." All she really wanted to do was rush home and open her purchases, but she wouldn't be able to benefit from them until Dean got home that evening, anyway. "Yes, okay. Just a quick one, though."

"No problem." Jeanette bustled into the kitchen and filled the kettle before switching it on. "So, what are you having?"

"Tea is fine, thanks. Milk, one sugar."

Then began a conversation that Lisa let go in one ear and out of the other. All she could think about was what she'd come to Jeanette's for in the first place, and what she was going to do when her other half got home. Put on some sexy underwear and get her arse spanked, hopefully.

Six o'clock could absolutely not come quickly enough. After dashing home from Jeanette's and opening the sealed bag containing her purchases, she'd taken everything out and examined them— deliberately leaving the spanking paddle until last—then put it all away. Only then did she regret her haste. Now she still had bloody hours before Dean would finish work, and therefore lots of time to fill. She ended up changing the bed and cleaning their bedroom before heading into the kitchen to cook something delicious for their evening meal. Something with lots of calories that would give them plenty of energy. Lisa chuckled to herself—Dean was definitely going to have a night to remember. And so was she.

About an hour before Dean was due home, Lisa went to get ready. She had a nice long shower, shaved and exfoliated, then slathered herself in her best body lotion before retrieving the new underwear set and hold-up stockings and lying them on the bed. She towel dried her body and hair before using the hairdryer to turn her still-damp locks into a mass of silky curls. Then she put on some deodorant and perfume, pulled on the slinky undergarments and wrapped her black satin robe around her, cinching the belt tightly around her waist.

By the time she got back downstairs, she had only minutes to spare. She checked on the food in the oven, noting with delight that it was almost ready, then sat down at the kitchen table to wait for Dean. Only a couple of minutes had passed when she heard the sound of his key in the door. It swung open and she watched as he opened his mouth to call out that he was home, then shut it abruptly when he saw she was sitting right there.

"Hi, sweetie," she said, moving out of the chair as gracefully as she could, then crossing the room and stretching to press a kiss to his lips. "Good day?"

She could hear the confusion in his voice as well as see it on his face when he replied, "Fine thank you, babe. What about you?" He looked her up and down, and his frown deepened. "Shit, are we supposed to be going out or something? What have I forgotten? Do I need to run and get ready?"

"No, no, no," she waved her hands. "Stop panicking. We're not going anywhere. Dinner's almost ready if you want to go and change into something more comfortable, though." She grinned, and the curve of her lips grew wider as she saw Dean glance at the oven, then back at her, his eyes growing darker with lust when he realised she was wearing stockings. "Can I pour you a drink while you're changing, babe?"

"That would be great. Wine, please. Whatever bottle you want to open is fine with me."

He flashed her a smile, then quickly headed upstairs.

Lisa popped open the first bottle she put her hand on in the fridge, then poured two glasses and set them on the table. Then she grabbed the plates from where they'd been warming on the top of the oven and put them on the worktop. Next, she pulled on her oven gloves. By the time she'd dished up the various parts of the meal and put the loaded plates on the table, Dean walked back in.

"Hey you," he said, moving behind her and slipping his arms around her waist, nuzzling into her neck and pressing a kiss to her skin. "Not that I'm complaining, but what's the occasion? I know it's not our anniversary."

"I know you know. You've never forgotten our anniversary, or anything like that. There isn't an occasion, other than I love you and felt like spoiling you."

"In that case, I'm going to take being spoiled, and be very grateful. Thank you, sweetheart." He kissed her neck again, then pulled away. "Anything I can do?"

"Yep. Sit your sweet arse at the table and enjoy your dinner."

"That," he said, with a playful slap to her bottom, "I can do."

They took their places, and Dean picked up his wine glass and held it towards her. "A toast," he said, his eyes gleaming, "to my beautiful wife, and the way she spoils me for no reason whatsoever. I'm a lucky man."

"You ain't seen nothin' yet," she replied, clinking her glass against his, then taking a sip. "Now eat."

He nodded and picked up his cutlery. They fell silent, with the exception of pleasurable moans and groans as the two of them enjoyed their meal.

"Phew. That was absolutely delicious, Lis. In fact, delicious isn't a strong enough word, but I can't think of a better one at the moment, so you'll just have to believe me."

'The noises you made while eating it were compliment enough for me. Though I have to say, it was bloody good, wasn't it?"

They laughed together, then Lisa drained the last of her wine and put the glass down.

"Another?" Dean asked.

"No, thanks. I've got a better idea."

"You do?"

She gave him a saucy wink, then directed her gaze to the

ceiling. "Want to go upstairs?"

"What a silly question! Want me to clear up, first?"

"Nah, screw it, I'll do it in the morning."

"You sure? I don't want you to think I'm letting you do everything."

"I'm sure. This was my treat. So just enjoy." She stood, and tugged the belt of her robe so the sides slipped open, giving a tantalising glimpse of what was beneath.

Dean's eyes almost fell out of his head. "Yes," he said, standing up so quickly his chair fell over, "I think I will enjoy." He took her hand and all but dragged her up the stairs and into the bedroom.

"So," he said, after drawing the curtains and closing the door, "what do you have planned for me now, my gorgeous wife?"

"More like the other way around, actually."

Dean frowned.

"I bought some stuff from that party I went to last week. This lot, for starters." She let the robe drop to the floor, revealing her lingerie-clad form. She hadn't put shoes on, despite knowing that would have sexed the look up a further notch, but only because she knew falling on her arse would undo all her good work. She'd never been one for heels.

"Um... I'm not sure what to say. Except think of every good, complimentary word in the English language and... that. I say again, I'm a very lucky man."

"But that's not all I bought."

"It's not?" His eyes widened, and he pressed a hand to his crotch. Things were clearly getting uncomfortable for him in the underwear region.

Lisa stifled a smirk. "No." Crossing to the dresser, she opened the top drawer, where she'd stashed the spanking paddle. She drew it out, deliberately holding it in front of her so Dean couldn't see it until she was ready. Closing the drawer, she then turned, moving her hand behind her this time. Moving towards her husband, she stood right in front of him, so their chests were almost brushing against one another. Then she reached around and pushed the paddle into his hand.

"I think you can work out the rest."

Dean lifted his arm and looked at what he held. His eyebrows almost disappeared into his hairline. He shifted his glance back to her. "You want me to use this on you?"

"Yes, please," she said, seeing no reason to beat about the bush. It had been on her mind ever since Frankie had whacked her in jest, and now she wanted to experience it for real, in a sexual situation which would have a proper payoff. An orgasmic one.

"Oh, okay. You know I've never done it before, don't you? So you'll have to tell me what to do."

"I haven't either, so I guess we'll have to learn together."

"Fair enough. How do you want to do it?"

"Maybe start off small? You get naked and sit on the chair, and I'll lie across your lap. Start with your hand to get me warmed up, then move onto the paddle."

"You know a lot for saying you've never done it before."

"The Internet is for more than just shopping, sweetheart."

He stuck out his tongue, then did as she said, dropping his discarded garments one by one into a pile at his feet. Then he walked—his erect cock bobbing—to the chair and sat down. "Okay," he said, beckoning to her, "I'm ready when you are."

Lisa grabbed the paddle from where Dean had left it on the edge of the bed and walked to him, dropping the implement next to the chair, then carefully positioning herself across his lap.

"Okay, babe. Just, um, go for it, I suppose."

"You don't wanna do any foreplay first, or anything?"

"I've been having mental foreplay ever since I ordered the bloody thing. I'm as ready as I'll ever be."

"If you say so. Just let me know if you want me to stop or I'm going too hard or something. I don't want to hurt you. I mean *really* hurt you, anyway. Obviously a bit of pain is the whole point." He chuckled.

"If I want you to slow down or not go so hard, I'll say amber. If I want you to stop I'll say red."

"Understood. Great idea, babe. God, this is so weird. Good weird, though. It's just I never thought I'd be spanking your arse."

"You're not, Dean. You're talking."

"Right, sorry. Amber and red, okay. I'm going for it." With that, he began to rub his hand across her bum cheeks, slowly at first, then faster.

Just as she was about to tell him to get on with it, she heard movement, then his palm cracked down on her arse. Purely on instinct, she yelped, even though the pain was already radiating across her skin and morphing into a pleasant burn. Immediately, the burn sent a heaviness to her groin, and, beneath her skimpy thong, she felt her labia swell. All that from one blow. She could hardly wait for more.

Fortunately, Dean didn't make her wait. Satisfied her yelp wasn't one of extreme agony, he smacked her other arse cheek. Then switched sides again. After a couple more tentative blows, he got into a rhythm, or maybe just felt more comfortable with what he was doing, because the spanks came thick and fast, and gradually got harder.

Lisa could scarcely believe the way her body was reacting. Far from hurting more each time a blow landed on her bottom, she grew more and more aroused. The harder the hits came, the better it felt, and before long she knew the gusset of her brand-new knickers was sodden. And they hadn't even kissed, never mind anything else. It was different, it was hot, and suddenly all she wanted to do was ride Dean until his teeth rattled and they both screamed out in climax. But he hadn't even used the paddle yet, and that was the whole point of the evening.

"Hey," she said loudly, trying to sound steady and confident, which proved incredibly difficult, given the hormones racing around her body and threatening to turn her into a puddle of blissed-out mush. "Want to swap to the paddle now? Give your hand a rest?"

Dean didn't speak, instead taking up the paddle.

It was only then that Lisa realised just how hard his cock was beneath her. She'd been so lost in her own enjoyment, her own lust, that she hadn't really given a thought to how this might be affecting her husband. Very favourably, it seemed.

He swept his free hand over her scorched buttocks, then replaced it with the paddle. The cool leather felt lovely against her tortured flesh, right up until Dean lifted it and brought it crashing back down upon her. It felt utterly different to the sensation of skin upon skin, but still totally delicious. And she knew he'd be able to beat her much harder with the implement than he would with his bare hands. So she encouraged him to do so.

"Are you sure? Your arse is already really red."

"And my pussy is already extremely wet."

"It is?"

His shaft twitched beneath her, and she grinned. Apparently Dean was as surprised at just how hot this experience was as she.

"Just do it, husband mine."

"O—okay." With that, there was a whoop as the paddle cut through the air and struck her buttocks.

She gasped, then groaned as the pain jangled across her nerves. Again and again, relatively gently, then more forcefully as Dean realised she could handle it, and wasn't shouting out any of the warning words they'd agreed on. Instead, an almost constant stream of blasphemy was tumbling from her lips as she disappeared increasingly further into her bliss. She was scarcely aware of her surroundings, and all she was sure of was her own body, and Dean's lap beneath her, his torso against her side, and the arm, wrist and hand that landed strike after strike on her white-hot cheeks.

After some time—she had no idea how long—Dean stopped. "I'm sorry," he said, dropping the paddle onto the carpet, "I've got to stop. My arm is aching like fuck and your arse is now more purple than red. I don't want to do any permanent damage."

"It's okay," she replied breathlessly, "I think I'm... oh, I dunno." She really didn't know, either. It was like her brain had disconnected, left her unable to focus on anything except what she was physically feeling. "Dean, please fuck me."

"Christ, I'd fucking love to. I'm not sure how I'm going to do it without hurting your bum, but I'm sure I'll figure something out."

As he carried her over to their bed and gently deposited her on the mattress, all she could think of was him inside her, fucking her, jerking and thrusting them both to orgasm.

Beyond that, there was nothing. There was only extreme pleasure brought on by her first spanking—after the party.

Clean/Dirty

I love pussy. Well, one in particular. My girl is so much more to me than just a pussy, but when we get in the mood she makes my cock so hard it hurts.

She's beautiful to me all the time, but she drives me particularly wild when she wears sexy little thongs. She pulls the stringy waistbands up above her jeans to tease me, so I know what she's wearing and I think about what's underneath.

I like to strip her naked, leaving her just in one of those teeny-tiny thongs. By this point I already have an erection straining desperately for release. She lies flat on her back on the bed and I part her thighs. More often than not, her pussy is wet and her juices have soaked through the material of her panties. I get harder still at that point, knowing that her gorgeous pussy is aroused and ready. For me.

I want to see it, taste it. But not yet. First I ask her to pull her thong tight into her groin. Not so much that it hurts, but enough that the material is tight to her skin, revealing her cunt's outline in all its glory. I gaze at the vision before me, material wedged up into her labia, and I want her.

I put out a hand to stroke her through the fabric, marvelling at how plump and soft she feels against my fingers. It sounds cheesy, but it makes me want to worship her cunt. I guess I do, already. I adore it, regularly.

I love to tease her, the way she does to me. I bury my head between her thighs and run my tongue up each side of that soaking gusset in turn. I want to eat her, desperately. But there is more fun to be had first. Much more.

Pushing her legs up towards her chest, I expose the delicate skin between her buttocks. The thong stretches taut across that forbidden hole. I want to stick my tongue there, too. But not yet.

I skate my tongue across her sensitive skin, around and across that sexy piece of underwear, never once touching what is underneath. I hold the backs of her thighs tightly to keep her from wriggling. She's trying; I feel her muscles contract beneath my palms and smile. Horny little wench.

Soon I cannot resist any longer. I hook one finger beneath her panties and pull them to one side, exposing her pink, glistening pussy and dark, tempting arsehole. As I gaze upon the perfection between her legs, I don't know where to start. Then instinct takes over and I bury my face between her thighs and my tongue in her slick folds.

She tastes divine. Sweet and tart at the same time; delicious. I want more. I slide my tongue into her hole; deep as it can go. Her juices flood my taste buds and my cock throbs. Flicking and teasing her, I dart in and out and all around her swollen pussy as she moans and wriggles beneath me. She's so wet now that it's trickling down her arse crack, lubricating that tight crinkle of flesh. I dive in.

My girl tenses up and squeals as my tongue invades her most private, forbidden place. I push inside, loving the feel of her rectal muscles giving way beneath my oral one. She clamps and twitches around me and more moans are followed by fresh juices sliding down towards my eager mouth. I lap them up, then move back up to the source.

She's so open and aroused now that it takes every ounce of self control I have not to pull out my cock and spear her on it. Her clit is swollen and distended, as big as it gets. And I haven't even touched her there yet. But I think she's waited long enough. I know I have.

Hooking my thumbs inside her labia, I separate them, exposing her further. Then I fasten my mouth onto her clit. She's so sensitive by now that she quickly starts thrashing around, and the horniest sounds I've ever heard spill from her lips. I suck at her swollen nub, delighting in the pleasure I'm giving her as she bucks and jerks beneath me. I know she can't be far from climax, so I move my hand down to her gaping hole and slide two fingers home.

She's so hot and wet it's like entering a tunnel of molten lava. Curling two fingers I begin to stroke her G-spot as I lick and suck at her clit. Seconds later, she hits her plateau and comes hard, her cunt clutching greedily at my fingers and soaking them in her juices. I hold still as she rides out her orgasm. When she's relaxed somewhat, I pull out and stuff my fingers into my mouth.

She watches me, a lazy smile on her face, as I lick and slurp every trace of her orgasm from my fingers. I don't want to waste a single drop of that precious nectar.

I smile back, because I know what comes next. Removing her teeny-tiny excuse for underwear, then stripping out of my clothes, I climb between her legs once more. She needs no more priming, her perfect pussy is ready for me. I sigh contentedly as I saw my cock up and down her slit, coating my shaft with her juices. It feels so good that I could almost come from this alone. My girl groans as my length pushes and rubs at her clit, then squeals as I enter her quickly after my down stroke.

The unexpected invasion makes her tense and twitch, her core gripping me tight. It feels incredible; a tight fist of lust wrapped around my cock, stroking me to orgasm. I brace myself on my hands and watch her face as I begin to pump in and out of her cunt. She reaches up to grab my arse cheeks, kneading and gripping them in her hands, using them to pull me deeper inside her. She's greedy, my girl; always wants more. And I'm more than willing to give it.

I'm buried inside her, my balls pressed tightly to her skin. Her swollen walls caress and cushion me and I want to stay there forever. But of course, neither of us will come that way, and we both know it. She reminds me by bucking her hips up at me, encouraging me to ride her.

I'll ride her, all right. I'll ride her until my teeth rattle. Accelerating, my hips thrust forward and back, my cock spearing her cunt, sending waves of sublime sensation through us both. I go as fast as my body will allow, deep and hard. Soon, I meet her eyes and know that she's ready.

Reaching between our bodies, my girl strums that delicious clit of hers and I immediately feel her tighten around me. I moan, the sensation bringing me close; closer. I feel her knuckles working away down there and soon, a breathy sigh issues from her mouth. She's coming.

The sigh quickly turns into a scream as her second climax rips through her body. She bows off the bed, then flops back down, her pussy spasming madly. I can't help it. She's milking me; I come. I force myself deeper inside her, then freeze as my cock starts spurting. I feel goose pimples cover my body, and the hairs on the back of my neck stand up as I release. I shiver with pleasure.

For some, this would mean the end. Or at least a lie down and a cuddle before round two. Not us. When I've regained enough strength in my arms and legs, I move so my face is between her thighs once more. This is the best part. Pulling apart her nether lips now reveals both our orgasms combined together, creating a sticky mess. And I'm just the man to clean it up.

I burrow my tongue inside her once more, licking up our

juices. It's an acquired taste, I'll give you that, but it does it for me. Salt and sea, tart, tangy, delicious. I lick and slurp and, just when I think I'm done, more seeps out of my girl's hot pussy. I clean up every last drop, lick until all that's left is one shiny, beautiful and glistening cunt.

By the time I'm finished, my cock is hard again. I manoeuvre her up on to all fours and spread her arse cheeks wide. Burying my tongue in her tight rear hole, I know it won't be long before we start making a mess again.

The taste of her arse, so different from that of her pussy, is equally delicious. Perhaps even more so, because it's so dirty, forbidden. I don't care. All I know is I love the feeling of my tongue spearing my girl's bum. She moans, pushes back onto my face, urging me deeper; she wants more.

I do too. Kneeling up, I slide my cock into her wet pussy once more, getting it nice and lubricated. When I'm satisfied, I pull out and line up the head of my cock with her arse. She's pushing, she wants it. I give it to her. Slowly but surely, I enter her back passage, almost impossibly tight around my shaft. She's moving, encouraging me. Soon I can't hold back and I thrust into her up to the hilt, then start fucking her in earnest.

The iron grip around my dick is delicious. She's screaming and bouncing on me; her hand between her legs, mashing her clit like there's no tomorrow. It's not going to take me long to come again, filling her arse full of my spunk.

I'm going to be cleaning up again, very soon. And I can't wait.

Crawl To Me

"So what *do* you want?" I asked, staring incredulously at the man who'd just confessed he thought our sex live was getting stale. It wasn't arrogance that brought on my surprise, but genuine shock. I'd thought we'd had it pretty damn good, to be honest. We'd tried as many positions from the Kama Sutra that were achievable for people that didn't practise yoga, played with toys, tried spanking and tying up... the list went on.

Jesse met my gaze, then shrugged.

"I don't know, Daniella. I just know that what we're doing now isn't... enough for me. I love you, I really do, but I just don't feel fulfilled in the bedroom."

The way he shrugged made it seem like it didn't matter to him. Like he was happy just to throw our relationship away, rather than reaching inside himself to work out what he *really* wanted. His seemingly nonchalant attitude sent a wave of anger through me so intense that I didn't know what I'd done until Jesse's head snapped back. He turned back to me, his eyes wide with shock and reached a hand up to rub his rapidly reddening cheek. My palm tingled.

Seconds later, the mood changed. And all because I couldn't take my eyes from his face. I watched as the shock disappeared from his expression and was replaced with something else. His nostrils flared, his eyes narrowed and his breath hitched. Unless I was totally mistaken, he was... aroused. A glance at his denim-clad crotch confirmed my suspicions.

A maelstrom of thoughts invaded my mind. I sorted through them as fast as I could until I found the one that made the most sense. He'd enjoyed the pain from where I'd slapped him. Interesting. I decided to carry on in the same vein and see where it went. If it turned out I was wrong and something else had turned him on, I'd probably never work it out. And if he didn't know what he wanted himself, how the hell was I meant to? However, if I was right then we could start playing a whole bunch of new games together and maybe save the relationship that was apparently waning through lack of sex. Or lack of *satisfactory* sex, according to Jesse.

I glared at him. "What the fuck do you mean, it's not enough anymore?"

He opened his mouth, but I quickly raised a finger to stop

him speaking. "I'm not finished. Though I'm eager to know why after all this time, I'm suddenly not enough for you."

I paused then, waiting for an answer. Instead I got something that fuelled my anger further. I got another shrug.

"Are you having a fucking laugh? You've thought about this enough to break up with me, but not enough to give me a fucking reason?" I couldn't help myself—I was livid. And if I was going to go through with my plan, it was now or never.

"Right," I said, "if that's how you feel, I obviously can't change your mind. But there's something I'd like to say first."

Jesse stiffened, clearly expecting some kind of onslaught of insults, or something. But I said no such thing. Instead, I barked, "Take off your clothes."

His eyes widened, but he did nothing.

I put my hands on my hips and raised my eyebrows. "It wasn't a request," I said, coolly. "It was an order. Do it. Now."

He soon realised what was happening, and I stood silently, triumphantly as he did as he was told. He shot me a couple of quizzical looks as he did it, perhaps expecting me to start laughing, having played a mean joke on him. But my expression remained stony and he continued stripping until he was completely naked. It was now blatantly obvious that I was barking up the right tree—his cock was rock hard and already had a bead of pre-cum at its tip.

I couldn't stop the smirk that tugged at the corners of my lips. Who would have thought it? Jesse liked to be dominated. After all this time together, he'd never even shown the slightest inkling that female domination was what interested him, turned him on. He'd spanked me, tied me up, ordered me around, and at the time had seemed to enjoy it. But perhaps he'd spent the entire time we'd played wishing that our roles were reversed.

Well, now he was going to get his wish. I looked him up and down, appraising him. Despite the bombshell he'd dropped, and how much it had pissed me off, I wasn't angry enough to be immune to his charms. He was an incredibly sexy man; tall, lithe and handsome. And now I was going to punish him. Granted, it was what he wanted, but I figured I could take my hurt feelings out on him and make myself feel better. So it was a win-win situation.

"Good," I said, bringing my gaze to his face, which wore an expression of bewilderment. But I didn't miss the fact that his eyes sparkled with lust. And of course, there was his bobbing cock, too, waving the banner for his arousal.

"Now, get down on your knees. Then press your forehead to the carpet and wait there until I say you can move."

I couldn't help being surprised when he did as I said, instantly and wordlessly. A rush of excitement crashed through my body, centring in on my groin, making my clit throb and my pussy lips swell. The power rush was intoxicating and horny. Perhaps there'd be more to this situation than punishing Jesse—maybe I'd enjoy it on its own merits. Maybe I was a Domme, and I just didn't know it. And I was perfectly happy to find out, one way or another.

I left Jesse where he was, looking every inch the submissive, with his head bowed, pressed to the floor. Somehow, I knew he wouldn't move. Apparently, this kind of thing got him off, so he'd probably still be there at midnight if I didn't give him the order to get up. The temptation tickled at the edges of my consciousness, but I pushed it away. No, I was trying to find out if this could save our relationship—doing something so extreme would be a *real* punishment, not a sexual one, and that wasn't what the game was about. This was about discovering something new about ourselves and our relationship, and whether it could keep us together. And maybe me taking my anger out on him. Just a little bit.

Heading into our bedroom, I stripped off my jeans, t-shirt, underwear and socks, then reached into our toy drawer to find something to wear that was more suitable for the situation. I retrieved the leather spanking paddle, since it sat at the top of the drawer, then continued digging around for something to wear. A PVC all-in-one soon appeared and I pulled it out. Holding it up, I decided that it would be the perfect outfit for my first try at being a Mistress. I'd always felt incredibly sexy in it, and being sexy was synonymous with being powerful. For me, at least.

I stood, closed the drawer, then moved over to the bed and dropped the items I'd found. But I wasn't quite ready to use them yet. First I needed to find the perfect fuck me shoes to go with the clingy outfit and the metal-studded paddle.

A quick rummage in my wardrobe unearthed a pair of platform stilettos. I put them on the bed, then grabbed the all-in-one and proceeded to put it on. Which was easier said than done. I didn't have the time to lube or talcum powder up, so I continued to fight the friction of the material against my naked skin. Eventually, I succeeded. I stood in front of the mirror and tweaked the edges of the outfit until it was in the right place. Then I sat down on the bed and pulled on the shoes. God, but they were some serious fuck me shoes. They were black patent, with the thick platform and the tall slim heel in scarlet patent. They were so hot, they made me want to fuck myself. Maybe I would—in front of Jesse. That would *really* piss him off.

Soon, I was all strapped into the shoes and ready to go. I grabbed the paddle and stood up. Twisted to have a last glance at myself in the mirror, gave a satisfactory nod and sauntered back into the living room, where Jesse remained in position. He couldn't see me, so I allowed myself a broad smile at this brand new turn of events. I stepped closer, and although my heels were on carpet, I must have made some kind of noise as I saw Jesse's back stiffen. My smile grew wider.

It was time to have some fun. I slapped the paddle into my palm, delighting in the sound it made in the quiet room. Jesse's muscles tensed and released—he obviously knew what was in store for him now, and was waiting in delicious anticipation. I idly wondered if I could make him come just by ordering him around and spanking him—without either of us touching his cock. I was willing to try and find out. Just maybe not today.

I moved so I was right next to his naked and prone body, then began to circle him, as an eagle would its prey. The whisper of my thighs against each another clearly let him know just how close I was, and I grinned as Jesse's body began to quiver with anticipation. Wow, this female domination thing seriously did get him off. I'd barely started yet, and he was already gagging for it. As I moved, I became aware that he wasn't the only one being turned on by the situation. My pussy grew wetter by the second, and my clit throbbed, a situation exacerbated by the rub and tug of the PVC suit against my groin.

I paced around Jesse a couple more times, trailing my arm so the leather paddle swept over his skin as I moved. He wriggled and twitched at the sensations, particularly when I passed by his bottom, touching the tip of the implement against his sensitive skin. I came to a halt in front of his head.

"Look at me," I commanded. Immediately, Jesse's head shot up. I bit back a grin when I saw how flushed he was. I hadn't laid a finger on him yet.

"Right," I continued, turning away from him, walking to the

other side of the room and perching on the edge of the sofa, "up on your hands and knees. Then crawl to me."

From my vantage point across the room, I could see his long, thick cock bobbing as he rushed to do as I said. A fresh trickle of juice leaked from my pussy at the sight. It was hardly surprising, though. I was a sucker for Jesse's dick and always had been. When we fucked, it stretched me to the point of pain and if we wanted to do it rough and fast, we had to find a position where its tip wouldn't knock painfully against my cervix. But despite that, its girth and quirky bend meant that it never failed to stimulate my G-spot; therefore I was quickly gushing and as a result, wet enough for more strenuous screwing.

I'd sure miss that cock if we split up.

By now, he was almost at the sofa. I looked down and gave him what I hoped was a menacing smile. "Good. Now eat my pussy. And if you don't make me come in less than five minutes, there'll be hell to pay."

A nervous look crossed Jesse's face. The best part was that he didn't know what I was going to be doing while he ate me out.

I moved so my arse was right at the very edge of the sofa and spread my legs. Jesse moved between them eagerly, and immediately pulled aside the material that covered my pussy. I held in a contented sigh as his tongue burrowed between my swollen labia and sought my clit. I was normally rather vocal when having sex, so it was easy for Jesse to know where he was right and where he was wrong, but this time, he was absolutely going to have to work for it.

Moving one hand to grab the leather paddle, I used the other to grip Jesse's hair; hard. I pulled his face tighter into my crotch, delighting in the sounds he made as he sucked in shaky breaths. He was so close to me that anything he could see would be blurry, so he closed his eyes. I smiled. That's exactly what I wanted him to do. Now my next move would shock the fucking hell out of him.

Trying hard not to move my body—alerting him that I was doing something—I stretched my arm as far as it would go over his back and down towards his arse. I worked out that with the length of my arm, and the extra inches afforded by the paddle I held, if I spanked him now it would land squarely at the top of his pale arse cheeks. Above the fleshiest part, but well below the area where it could be dangerous due to the proximity of his kidneys.

I leaned forward a little more, then brought my arm down hard. The satisfying sound permeated the air, rapidly followed by a grunt from Jesse.

"Hey," I said, pulling on his hair. "Get on with it. You have less than four minutes. And the longer it takes you to make me come, the harder I'm going to spank you."

In truth, I had no idea how long he'd been going down on me. But I wasn't about to tell him that.

My words renewed his vigour, and he licked and sucked at my pussy until I had to bite my lip with the effort of keeping quiet. Luckily I had the spanking to help divert my concentration elsewhere, and keep my climax at bay a little longer. I continued to swipe at Jesse's bottom, laying thick pink stripes across his white skin. I swung harder and harder, turning the pink blush redder and redder until finally, with two fingers pressing against my G-spot and his lips pursed around my swollen clit, Jesse made me come.

Dropping the paddle, I tangled my other hand into Jesse's hair and ground and writhed against his face as my orgasm burned through my body like a wildfire. Soon, I was too sensitive and I pushed him roughly away, sending him sprawling to the floor as I flopped back into the soft cushions of the sofa. The shockwaves continued to rock me, and my cunt clenched at thin air a few more times as I rode out the rush of pleasure. I breathed heavily until I came fully back to myself. Normally, this would be the point where we'd either cuddle or carry on playing. And, this time, we were definitely going to carry on playing.

"Get up," I snapped, reaching down to pull the crotch of the bodysuit back to where it was supposed to be and sitting up straight.

He scrambled back to his hands and knees, then, clearly unsure as to whether he was meant to stay there or stand up, he looked at me questioningly.

"Stay where you are," I said coldly, standing up and looking down at him from the towering height achieved by the fuck me shoes. "I have more plans for you. In fact, you can do something for me right now, right where you are. Lick my shoes."

I had no idea whether my command would be pushing it one step too far, but Jesse's sudden lurch at my feet showed that it wasn't. In an almost crazed fashion, he ran his tongue along the platform soles, up across the patent leather that covered my toes, and back down the heel. He did this over and over, swapping feet until his breathing became laboured. I knew damn well it wasn't from exertion, so the only sensible conclusion was that this particular method of Mistress-worship was driving him crazy. Completely and utterly crazy.

I stepped back. "Kneel, so I can look at you."

Jesse knelt up, which meant I could see his torso, and more importantly, his cock. I raised an eyebrow. The end of his prick and part of his stomach were covered in pre-cum. There was so much of the stuff that it looked like he'd had a mini-climax. But I knew he hadn't; I'd have been able to tell.

"Well," I said, "it certainly seems like you're enjoying yourself. Do you like being my slave?"

I hadn't really thought about Jesse being my slave until that very moment. But the more I thought about it, the more I realised that that's exactly what he was. For the time being, at least. I decided to push harder. I sat back down on the sofa and beckoned to him. "Remove my shoes. Then worship my feet again."

We'd never done foot play before, so I had no idea if it would do anything for me. But given the fact that dominating him had my pussy wet and my nipples pressing against the material of the bodysuit, I suspected that it would. Probably the more things I told him to do—providing he complied, of course—the more aroused I would become.

Wordlessly, Jesse took off my shoes—which took him longer than it should have done due to his trembling fingers—and rubbed and stroked my feet for a few seconds before lowering his head to the toes of my right foot. I tried hard not to tense up; I had no idea if this was going to be ticklish, kinky, or disgusting, and my body wanted to show my hesitance. But I didn't allow it—this was about tormenting Jesse, although he was enjoying it, and seeing how far he would go in pursuit of his passion for submission.

Submission. When I thought about it, about the word, about everything it meant, a thrill ran through my body. When Jesse and I had played in the past with me being the one tied down, teased, tormented, it had turned me on, but not because I was being submissive. It was just because it felt good. But Jesse clearly got off on being topped, and judging by the way I was happily ordering him around and steadily getting wetter and hornier, I was getting revved up over being dominant.

Wow, if Jesse had only had the guts to speak up about his

deepest, darkest fantasy before, we could have been playing kinky games for months; years.

But it didn't matter. What mattered was that we were playing now, and we'd both discovered new sides of ourselves. Sides that got us seriously hot under the collar, and that I suspected would become more permanent parts of our lives. I hoped so, anyway. If this was the way to save our relationship, then I was all for it. And at the rate we were going, we were going to be enjoying seriously hot and kinky sex with one another until we were old and grey.

For now, though, my PVC-clad body grew hotter and hotter as Jesse's agile tongue flicked between my toes, over the underside of my foot, around my heel, up across my ankle and back over the arch of my foot and down to my toes once more. Then he pulled my big toe into his mouth and began to suck it—mimicking fellatio. The sensation itself was more pleasant than arousing, but the intense power trip had me writhing in my seat and resisting the temptation to throw Jesse onto his back and ride his cock until we both exploded. I would definitely be doing just that some time in the near future, but not just yet.

I continued to watch Jesse worship my feet, and grinned like the Cheshire Cat. What would I ask him to do next? No, not ask him. *Command* him. I wrapped my mind around the words and phrases a Mistress would use and stored them in the forefront of my mind, ready to pull them out when they were needed.

That time happened to be sooner rather than later. My need to be fucked was growing stronger by the second, and I knew that I wouldn't be able to play around much longer without satiating that craving. So I came to the conclusion that one more form of exquisite torture was in order for my new slave before I granted him a good fucking.

"Slave," I said calmly, waiting for him to stop what he was doing and look at me. "Help me up. I have something else I'd like you to do."

Jesse disengaged from my peds and stood, reaching down to grab my hands and pull me up off the sofa. I gave him a nod of thanks, then issued my next command. "Now bend over the sofa, with your arse in the air. I'm going to give you a seeing to. And you absolutely, categorically, do not have my permission to come. You will come only when I say so. Understood?"

Immediately, he did as he was told, and the words "Yes,

Mistress" were issued from his new position. My cunt jolted—I liked being called Mistress.

"Good." I grabbed the leather paddle and swooped it through the air a few times, enjoying the noise it made. Not to mention the fact that it would tease Jesse terribly, being able to hear the implement and not knowing when it would strike him.

I was eager to get going, so I didn't make him wait long. I moved into a prime position behind him, smirking as I observed the fading marks I'd left on his bum earlier. They were nothing compared to what he was going to get now, though. He'd pay for his supposed indecision, which was, in fact, his cowardice. His inability to own up to what he really wanted. He was damn lucky I'd picked up on it, otherwise he could have ended up dissatisfied and potentially lonely for the rest of his life. The fact that I'd also discovered a dominant side to myself was by the by. This was about him; about his new submissive persona and starting off our new games as we meant to go on. Or how *I* meant to go on, anyway. Jesse wouldn't really have a choice in the matter.

The thought made me laugh, and at the same time I aimed and landed the first blow on his right buttock. In an interesting show of perfect submission, he flinched only slightly, and the only sound he made was sucking in a sharp breath. I barely gave him time to absorb the first blow before I laid the second one on him, and the third. I continued to spank him, alternating arse cheeks and areas until the whole of his bum and upper thighs were a glowing mass of firm flesh.

It was then, as I stood admiring my handiwork that I thought of a way that I could feel that glorious cock in my pussy and still be inflicting pain on my new obedient fuck toy. I tossed the paddle onto the sofa, then stroked my fingers down the red hot cheeks before me. A tiny sigh came from Jesse's lips.

I gave an evil grin, then, instead of stroking him again, I curled my fingers and drew my nails across his skin. I didn't need to press on hard—he was already in pain and he winced as I clawed at his reddened arse a few times, before grabbing his arm and tugging him upright. "Get on your back."

Jesse looked down at the carpet and then up at me. He kept his expression completely neutral, but I was sure he knew what I was up to. Doing as I asked, he lay down on his back and waited for my next instruction. There wasn't one. Instead, I struggled—completely ungracefully—back out of the PVC body suit and tossed it next to the paddle on the sofa.

I straddled him and stayed where I was for a few seconds, affording him the view up my body; my smooth legs, equally smooth pussy, slightly rounded tummy, pert and swollen tits and finally the expectant expression on my face.

"Are you ready, slave?"

He nodded vehemently, then suddenly remembered his place. "Yes. Yes please, Mistress."

I smirked, and lowered myself to my knees, still astride him. I reached down and grasped his eager cock, which was still sticky with pre-cum and aimed it at my opening. Quickly, I dropped onto it, though not all the way. I wasn't ready to take his full length, yet. I hovered, with most of Jesse's dick filling my pussy for a few seconds, before starting to ride him. I rolled my hips, knowing the movement would shift his body against the floor, and that the rough fibres of the carpet would abrade his flaming skin.

Grinning, I leaned back and gripped his thighs for leverage before picking up my pace. The position was perfect for me; I got to control the speed and depth of the thrusts—ideal with a cock as long as Jesse's—and my increasingly fast hip jerks meant I could inflict pain on his tortured bottom at the same time I was greedily and selfishly taking pleasure for myself.

"Stroke my clit," I barked, continuing to fuck him as hard and as fast as I could go without hurting one of us. Hurting in the bad way, that is. The pain Jesse was experiencing was clearly in the very good way, as his cock was as hard as I'd ever felt it. It stretched and pounded my cunt; manipulating my G-spot. Delicious.

His fingertips on my clit added another dimension to my already intense pleasure and within seconds I'd adjusted my position so my hands were pressed to his chest, my nails digging into his pecs. I stared deep into his eyes as I rocked myself to climax—with the help of his hand, of course—and when I felt the waves of pleasure begin to overtake my body, I clenched my fingers harder. His harsh intake of breath sent me over the edge, and I grunted and groaned as my climax hit.

I purposely kept my eyes open in order to see Jesse's reaction. As my pussy gripped and released, gripped and released his cock, I could see the look of intense concentration on his face as he tried his best not to come. Thankfully for him, the delicious pleasure that was racing through my body made me feel more generous.

"Okay," I said, giving a small smile, "you may come."

Almost as soon as the words left my lips, his entire body tensed beneath me and he reached up to grip my hips. He let out an animalistic roar and his cock began to twitch and leap as he emptied his balls inside me. I simply clung on to him, swaying happily as my own pleasure waned, watching his face go through a variety of expressions from overcome to utterly blissed out.

Normally I would have snuggled up to him now and enjoyed some intimacy as our respective orgasms made us sleepy and supremely satiated. Instead, I waited until he had come back to himself and sat up, looking down at his face.

"So, what do you think, Jesse? Are our new games enough for you now?" I spoke the words lightly, and smiled sweetly.

But it was clear that Jesse sensed the sarcasm—and therefore danger—beneath the happy, carefree veneer. He gulped; actually gulped—I heard the noise and saw his Adam's apple move up and down.

"Umm..." his eyes moved around wildly, as if he was desperately seeking the right answer to my question, and wondering if it was some kind of trick. Realising he was trapped, physically and otherwise, he opened his mouth. But not fast enough.

"Answer me! And no bullshit. It's a simple yes or no answer. I don't want any of that 'I don't know' crap."

He flinched. Gulped again, then looked at me earnestly. "Yes, the answer is yes. If you'll have me... Mistress."

Bingo. I certainly hadn't started the day with the intention to become my boyfriend's Mistress, but it was a result I was more than happy with. Especially since it meant our relationship would survive, and be even better than before.

About the Author

Lucy Felthouse is a very busy woman! She writes erotica and erotic romance in a variety of subgenres and pairings, and has over 100 publications to her name, with many more in the pipeline. These include several editions of Best Bondage Erotica, Best Women's Erotica 2013 and Best Erotic Romance 2014. Another string to her bow is editing, and she has edited and co-edited a number of anthologies, and also edits for a small publishing house. She owns Erotica For All, is book editor for Cliterati, and is one eighth of The Brit Babes.

Find out more about her and her books at the following links, and be sure to subscribe to her newsletter to make sure you don't miss out on the latest news, and a monthly giveaway.

Website: http://www.lucyfelthouse.co.uk
Facebook: http://www.facebook.com/lucyfelthousewriter
Twitter: http://www.twitter.com/cw1985
Goodreads: http://www.goodreads.com/cw1985
Pinterest: http://www.pinterest.com/cw1985
Newsletter: http://eepurl.com/gMQb9
The Brit Babes: http://www.thebritbabes.co.uk
The Brit Babes Street Team:
http://www.thebritbabes.co.uk/p/street-team.html
The Brit Babes on Facebook:
http://www.facebook.com/8britbabes
The Brit Babes on Twitter: http://www.twitter.com/8britbabes

Printed in Great Britain
by Amazon

19356937R00088

MULTI-ORGASMIC
A COLLECTION OF EROTIC SHORT STORIES

From the pen of award-winning erotica author Lucy Felthouse comes a collection of short stories and flash fiction sure to hit the spot.

There's something for everyone nestling between the pages of this sexy anthology. From spanking to voyeurism, bondage to pegging, solo loving to ménage, with a sprinkling of femdom, maledom and magic, fans of M/F erotic stories will soon discover why this book is described as multi-orgasmic.

Enjoy twenty one titillating tales, over 52,000 words of naughtiness packed into one steamy read.

Please note: Many of the stories in this book have been previously published in anthologies and online but three of the tales are brand new and never-seen-before!

"Whew! The ice maker is empty, my fan-wielding hand is exhausted and I'm already looking forward to the next group of Felthouse erotic stories. I have read many of her stories over the years, and always enjoy them. Multi-Orgasmic shows too many different kinds of eroticism to settle on any one. Suffice it to say you'll love them all, as I did."
5 out of 5, Manic Readers

ISBN 9781508702948

90000 >

9 781508 702948

√(w)o Bits

Loves, losses, and lenses

Melissa Zoller